CHIGGERS

PAUL HUGHES

Copyright ©Paul Hughes
2024 All rights reserved
This edition published in 2024
This is a work of fiction and any resemblance to people living or deceased is purely coincidental. No part of this publication may be reproduced or transmitted, in any form or by any means, without permission of the author

1

The light illuminated Pete as he selected a cold one from the innards of his old fridge. Then the phone rang insistently.
"What now!" He thought. He snatched it from its cradle and barked into it. "Yea! Who is it!"
"Pete, its Jack – Sheraton Chemicals" Came the reply.
"Hi Jack, sorry for that. What can I do for you?"
"I hate to ask you, but we cannot get anyone at such short notice. We got a load of disposables that have to reach the harbour in time to be loaded up and has to be there by 5.00pm latest!"
"Fuck me Jack its 1.30pm now! "
"There's a grand in it for you if you can do it? I am fucking desperate man!" Jack pleaded.
"Okay, a grand it is! I am setting off now so get them on pallets and ready to load!"
"You lifesaver!"

"Fuck off I am just doing it for the money!" He laughed.

Pete Tremayne jumped into his truck and turned the key. At first it coughed and wheezed and finally roared into life. Tremayne Hauliers had been in existence since Pete's Grand Pappy had started ferrying moonshine across the State line. Now it was a legal entity and Pete was very proud of his reputation for delivering the goods, for a good price and on time. In fact, that was the slogan he had painted on his truck.

2

Calico County was 20 miles from Sheraton Chemicals and Pete kept his foot on the gas all the way. He wanted to get this job done so he could get back to his wife and daughter Sophie. Afterall Sophie was having a 16th birthday celebration, and it was THE most important date in Pete's calendar.

    Pete being Pete never thought about looking after his trucks. If it ran it ran. Why mess with it, get as much money from it as you can was his motto. Okay he would keep the tyres renewed but they would be decent looking to the casual eye that may be turned in his direction from Sheriff Wilbur Deeds or his Deputy Jimmy Johnson.

    He arrived at the Sheraton Chemical Plant in record time and backed up to the loading dock where

Jack Swenson the supervisor was waiting with a pallet truck ready to load the cargo, Pete dropped his tailgate and loading began. He noted that there were eight yellow barrels with some strange looking symbols on the side and the lids had been welded in place.

"Take it easy with this load Pete, they ain't gonna take too kindly to being bumped a lot!"

"Just make sure they are lashed in real tight Jack and let me do the rest?"

Jack handed Pete the final paperwork and waved him off. "Don't forget the name of the ship is the Lady Durham and she sails with the tide at 5.00pm! No dilly dallying ya hear?" His words were fading fast as Pete revved the truck, before he raised a handout of his window and drove off knitting his brows as he took a quick glance at his watch.

"Damn they took 45 minutes to load me up and that will take some time to make up! If I take the highway it will take me out of my way and add time I don't have" He cursed.

Pete remembered a dirt road that was little used which went past the old Harper Mill near Breenville that would catch up with highway 101 that would save him some considerable time. The only catch was – if it was still passable?

Well, too late to worry he thought and sped off to the nearest off ramp.

A couple of miles down the road he found what he was looking for and it seemed to be wide enough for the truck to fit. Branches of overgrown trees brushed past in a confusion of sound.

He drove like a man possessed, his thoughts of getting a lot of money for an easy job occupied his attention. He took his mind off the road for a moment and missed the stump that grew at the side of the deserted road. There was a sudden bang as he hit it and a rusted bolt on the track rod sheared right off.

The steering wheel bucked like a mad bull in his hand, but the truck just rocketed on, heading for a gap in the trees. At last he thought that lady luck was on his side but as the trees parted, he saw he was heading for the lake. What Pete never saw was a tree looking like a knight, his lance raised, and the point levelled as it smashed the wind shield and pinned him to his seat as it entered between his ribs and punctured his lung. He tried to stand on the brakes, but the branch had pushed him too far back into his seat.

The impact shattered both the branch and swung the truck sideways, the tail flipped, and drums catapulted, snapping the rope lashings like thread. One smashing its way into the undergrowth, where it lay on its side with a large crack around a faulty weld line. The truck stopped miraculously perched on a clay bank. It had been raining the night before and the bank was slick with mud, the remaining barrels slid to the side and the sudden shift in weight tipped the truck over.

    Pete felt the sudden movement of his toxic load. Blood bubbled and frothed from his mouth and nose from his internal injuries. His breathing became jerky and spasmodic. His last thought was of his family and at least he wasn't going to drown as he passed with one last gurgling breath.

Pieces of clay came adrift under the weight of the truck in large chunks and the vehicle started to move again. The truck appeared to be in slow motion as it started to tumble and roll, finally sliding down the bank into the cold dark waters of the lake causing the barrels to jostle with each other, as they worked themselves loose and started buckling under the pressure of the water as more and more cracks appeared in their welds.

    As the truck and its driver slowly sank, a greenish black sludge oozed from the barrels continuously frothing and boiling up from the lake bottom where they popped and released their misty content into the atmosphere.

3

The Captain of the Lady Durham put in a phone call to Jack Swenson at 5.01.
"Where is the load Jack?"
"Pete Tremayne should have been there by now? He is always reliable and its unlike him to not finish a job!" Jack was perplexed.
"I gotta go the tide is up!"
"Ok, if you must? If he turns up, I am docking him for missing the boat!" Jack replied.

***

Pete's wife Ellie was sitting at the table that held a birthday spread and watched a tearful Sophie sob into her folded arms.

Ellie had begged Pete not to go, to let someone else do it but he promised he would be back in time and there weren't too many opportunities to make this much money for a quick job. She reluctantly agreed to let him go but deep down she had felt uneasy about it. It had seemed so furtive and why such a high price to do a job that Pete did at half the price.

Ten pm came and went with no sight or sound of Pete, so Sophie dragged herself to bed. Ellie laid on the couch and dozed off but was awoken when the alarm screamed in her head, only for her to realise that Pete had not come home, and it was now 6.30 am. Worried she called Sheraton Chemicals to enquire if Pete had arrived back there and the receptionist went to find someone who might know only to return and inform her that no one had seen him after he had left with his load. Upon hearing no one had seen him since he left, she hung up and instantly called Sheriff Deeds and reported him missing. He made a mental note of it and said he would travel the route Pete would have used in the hope that it was a simple breakdown.
***
Wilbur shook himself awake and made himself a fresh coffee.

He knew that Pete's truck was not in the best of health. He chuckled to himself as he thought of it.

Realised he was alone and solemnly climbed into his uniform pants and shirt and buckled on his official gun-belt. Sipping his coffee, he sat at his desk and wrote out the details that Ellie had given him. Halfway down his cup, he decided that he should go and investigate.

Wilbur was a silver haired lawyer who had retired to Calico county and loved it as soon as he had arrived a mere 15 years previously.

The Sheriff before him had passed away and the town had canvassed the area for a replacement. Fortunately, or unfortunately Wilbur put his name forward as a joke not expecting it to be given to him there and then. He suddenly realised that no one else had offered to do the job. It was apparently to be the same come election time. He had wanted to step down after a couple of terms, but the townsfolk didn't want him to leave.

He picked up his Stetson and dropped it onto his head where it rested at a somewhat rakish angle. Looked at himself in the mirror and felt good.

He eased himself into the old Dodge that came with the job and started it up. The engine purred and he eased off the handbrake before putting it in gear and headed to Sheraton Chemicals where Pete's journey began.

Upon arrival at Sheraton chemicals Wilbur was shown into Jack's office and he sat down, his hat in his hands. "So, tell me about Pete and this late job Ellie mentioned?"

Jack flushed red; he hadn't realised that Ellie knew about it, "Eh, well it was a rush job, a delivery of parts to the Captain of the Lady Durham!" He stammered.

"Important parts, were they?" Wilbur persisted.

"Yea! It was for the engine I believe!" Jack felt his collar tightening.

"Hmm, strange that because the ship sailed right on time! If these parts were so important, surely they couldn't sail on time then?" Wilbur watched Swenson closely. He knew he was lying; he had been a lawyer and dealt with people who lied for a living.

He watched Swenson squirming, like a worm on a hook.

"Okay Sheriff, I'll come clean it wasn't parts – it was barrels of waste chemicals that were to be disposed of somewhere out at sea in the deepest part." Swenson sat back relieved that he had told the truth. "The suits wanted it gone and left it up to me to arrange its disappearance – safely, you understand!"

Wilbur got up slowly and put on his hat.

"You will be held to account for this illegal dumping Swenson, it's up to the courts to decide. At the

moment I am only interested in the disappearance of Peter Tremayne, citizen of Calico County. If you hear anything call me – day or night ya hear?"
"Sure, thing Sheriff, I will." Said Swenson nervously.

Back in the car, Wilbur tried a few scenarios in his mind. Had Pete realised what he was carrying and tried to hide it. Did he take it back and was killed to prevent him talking?

Or has he just broken down and is waiting for someone to come by? The last one he sincerely hoped was the best option.

4

Route 101 to the harbour was a long boring road and Wilbur scanned every inch of it. He looked for any signs of an accident, spillages, skid marks, torn bushes, disturbed dirt banks.
Nothing jumped out at him.
He stopped on the roadside and stretched his legs. He was only a few miles away from the harbour and after a few minutes got back in his car and drove to the harbour.
He spotted an old guy sitting on a bench and wandered over to him. "Been here long?"
"Here all the time! Can't sleep so I come out to listen to the waves, kinda nice and peaceful and then back home to bed."

"Didn't happen to see a young feller with an old truck that had Tremayne on the side here last night? Would have been unloading for a ship called Lady Durham?"
"Nope! Sorry! No trucks here last night or this morning! Cos, I had a real bad night, it's the old rheumatism in my legs and back, keeps me up most nights."
"Thanks, old timer!"
"Hell, you look as old as me Sheriff. He laughed and coughed.
Wilbur laughed with him.

So back to square one. The mystery of the disappearing truck and driver and a mysterious load.

The Sheriff headed back to his office and filed a missing person report. He also called Ellie to let her know that he was unsuccessful in finding where Pete was and that there had been no clues as to where he had gone.

Ten weeks passed and a hiker appeared in the Sheriff's outer office. He had been hiking down the Harper Mill road and noticed the damaged trees and a yellow barrel that had been lying on its side on the clay bank. There was a strange smell in the air and the water of the lake had a thick scum floating on the top. Deputy Jimmy Johnson started making out the report and as soon as Wilbur heard the words yellow barrel he jumped up from his chair and read the hiker's report over Jimmy's shoulder.

"Did you notice anything else? Like a truck anywhere?" He asked.
"No! Just this weird barrel of gunge oozing out, it had spread out across the lake. Probably killed all the fish in there" He said sadly.
"Never was any fish in that lake son! I tried fishing in there when I first came to town. It was only man made to operate the Old Mill."
"Ok Jimmy, take Mr? "He paused.
"Hepworth, Sheriff!"
"Mr Hepworth to Harper lake and the place where he saw the leaking barrel. I am going to call in an expert on chemicals to handle it as soon as I find out what it is. And do not touch anything out there just note where it is, ok?" Wilbur said as he turned back to his office and shut the door.

Jimmy, and Mr Hepworth got into the pickup and drove off to Harper Lake. Upon arriving they got out of the pickup and walked a short way down the road. Overgrown trees were blocking the road and Jimmy noticed a shiny object on the trail near a stump. He picked it up and turned it over in his hand. It was rusty in parts but where it was shiny meant that it had sheared off. He knew that it was from a vehicle, and he also figured it was a broken track end.

They approached the gap and Hepworth pointed to where the yellow barrel lay. There was a very distinct smell coming from the leaking material and it caught in their throat making them cough for a moment.

Jimmy looked at the surface of the lake, which was frothing, and a fine fog hovered above it. He thought he saw something moving in the water but remembered Sheriff Deeds saying there was no fish in the lake. As he looked harder, he swore he could see something moving.

Easy to fool your eyes he thought as he approached the lake through some long grass for a closer inspection before he stopped and looked down at his uniform and noticed hundreds of tiny red spider-like creatures crawling all over him. They wandered up over his boots and into his socks, his skin itching all over, the creatures were biting him around his collar and up his sleeves as he tried frantically to brush them off. But as he removed some, thousands more came. They appeared in droves. More and more biting, he could feel them sucking his blood. He ran back to the pickup and tried to call Sheriff Deeds on the radio but there was no reception – no signal.

Hepworth was brushing frantically at the creatures too. As more creatures latched on to their skin, he noticed the newer ones were larger and they seemed to be getting bigger as each new wave hit them. The grass was heaving with millions of the creatures.

Gradually, they filled up their eyes, then their mouths filled when they tried to scream, and tiny pincers tore at their skin leaving a bloody mess. The creatures sucked the blood from their bones leaving an empty husk with clothing that hung loosely over a skeletal frame which suggested that they were once human.

5

"Sheraton Chemicals? Sheriff Wilbur Deeds here."
"Hi Sheriff Deeds, Gina Washington receptionist here what can I do for you?" She trilled.
"Who is the main man down there that knows about chemical handling?"
"Er! Why I guess that would be Elmer, I mean Dr Elmer Creed, he is our top scientist here in the laboratory?"
"Put me through to him straightaway darling!"
"I can't do that, Sheriff, he is not to be disturbed while doing an important experiment, I was told."
"Well, you tell him that if he doesn't shift his ass, I will be coming down there with a warrant for his arrest for illegal dumping of dangerous chemicals! Ya hear me?"

"Oh, er yes Sheriff, right away, Sheriff, let me put you on hold for a moment while I get him!" Gina stuttered, not used to the kind of tone that Wilbur had spoken to her.

"Dr Creed! Elmer, the County Sheriff is on the other line and if you don't talk to him, he says he is gonna arrest you! Says its important you talk?"
"Okay Gina put him on!"
"Hello! Dr Creed here, what's your problem Sheriff?"
"Listen here you panty waist. I have a problem of which no doubt you are at the top of it. Some nasty chemicals have been dumped into Harper Mill Lake. And I want to know what it is and how to get the damn stuff out of it!" Wilbur shouted.
"Sheriff Deeds calm down sir, I haven't a clue what you are talking about! I was here all day I never dumped any chemicals!" Creed replied.
"You, sorry sonofabitch I never said you physically dumped those chemicals, but they are your Company's property, seeing as you are the only sons of bitches that deal with that shit! So, I want to know what the hell it is, I am going to be dealing with! And you my slippery little friend are going to be my consultant and I use that term lightly. Cos I can close

you bastards down quicker than a skunk would clear a bar!"

Dr Creed knew by the Sheriff's tone of voice that he had to keep on the right side of him as he had heard that Wilbur Deeds had many friends in high places. "Okay Sheriff, I will be at your office in say – half hour?"
"Better be quick or there will be due process getting started." Wilbur slammed the phone down and looked at it angrily daring it to ring. Strange though he had expected his deputy to get in touch with him with some details. Then he realised that there was a poor signal at Harper Mill.

Dr Creed drove as fast as he dared. He didn't want to get ticketed for speeding. Although, he could use the excuse that it was an emergency for the Sheriff. This thought cheered him a little, but he felt very uneasy over the reason he was being summoned to the Sheriff's office.

He tried to think up various excuses as to why it had been dumped in the lake, but nothing came to mind. After all he had given the job to Swenson, and it was to be placed aboard a ship bound for the open sea. For every reason he could think of more questions formed instead.

Creed thought about the Company's experiment. The project was supposed to be for a solution to end third world starvation by creating disease and insect free crops. Each batch of chemical formula was tried and tested and all failures to be disposed of and usually in the deepest part of the ocean. This latest batch was faulty, the formula had added growth hormone and microbes that proved to be toxic in acidic soil. But Chemicals in this combination gave off irritating fumes and reacted with water in a volatile manner.

Dr Creed pulled up outside Wilbur's office. He thrust his attaché case under his arm and went in.

"Dr Creed!" Wilbur smiled and held out his hand. Elmer was taken aback but responded by accepting and shaking it strongly.

"Sorry, I had to use my lawyer voice to get you here, but I had to get your attention on this situation! Take a seat!"

"Well you certainly got my attention Sheriff! So, what is the problem?"

"Okay, I have a missing driver and his truck, said truck was alleged to have been loaded with some chemicals in a yellow drum with some sort of markings on it."

"Hold it their Sheriff you said yellow drums" Creed leaned forward in his chair, "Dear Lord, so that was what happened to Pete Tremayne's load."

"Looks like he couldn't make the ship and so he dumped it in Harper Mill Lake!"

"No sir! You are suggesting that Pete Tremayne dumped that load. Well not according to a witness that said it looked like Pete went off the track into the lake and a drum was dumped on the bank."

"Well I guess I owe you an apology there. And to inform you that this stuff is highly toxic to all life forms, is extremely volatile meaning it can explode given the right conditions."

"What are the conditions?"

"When in contact with water it forms a gas, which is poisonous to any life form as I said. If the gas is present in a large amount it can be ignited basically!"

"Ok so the best thing to do is retrieve the drum on the bank and ignite the gas in the lake? Okay sounds like a plan!" Wilbur made a motion to get up, but Creed stopped him.

"First, I have to go and get a couple of Hazmat suits because you won't be able to breathe around there!"

"Oh no! My Deputy and the witness are up there observing the site!" Wilbur sprang up from his chair.

"I am afraid it may be too late for them the gas will have formed and spread around." Dr Creed left Wilbur looking ashen as he thought about young Jimmy Johnson and the Hepworth guy. Deep down he hoped that they were alright and that they were keeping an eye on things till he and the expert got there.

Soon Dr Creed returned with two bright yellow suits that looked like Quasimodo had modelled for them but as he explained that was to accommodate the tanks of compressed air they needed to breathe while inside the suits. They were discussing their strategy when a breathless man in faded blue dungarees ran in. In between heaving breaths, he said his name was Dan Brown and he had a dairy farm over near Harper Mill. Some of his cows had been bitten by some huge insect before he threw a burned corpse on Wilbur's desk.

"This is the fucker I took off one of my cows!" He stood and looked at them both.

Wilbur examined it closely, it had curved jaws and appeared to have a bloated abdomen the oddest thing about it was its size, it measured a full five inches from its jaws to its end of its body. Dr Creed looked long and hard at it and suddenly gasped in recognition.

"Do you know what this is?" He spoke.
"No, I am a city boy never seen anything like this before!" Said Wilbur.

"No good asking me I ain't seen anything like it either!" Said the farmer.

"It's a Chigger but a gigantic one. They usually hide in the long grass, and at a guess there is plenty of that around the lake, they wait for an animal to come by jump on and suck a little blood out then drop off or you burn em off or maybe use a bit of alcohol to pour on them. How did you get this off the cow?"

"I used my weed burner and singed the bastard enough for it to curl up stone dead."

"Chiggers are usually so tiny and like red dots but this one – oh boy he certainly has grown, and I think we have a problem Sheriff. A far bigger one than we thought pardon the pun! The chemical formula we made has created them and they are growing exponentially that means they have been growing over these past ten weeks at a fantastic rate. We better get them stopped before they get any bigger." He continued, "and we better call in the National Guard too!"

Wilbur rang the local area Guard and informed them of their emergency. At first, they thought it was a joke but something in Wilbur's tone suggested otherwise. The Guard were mobilised.

Wilbur picked up a Hazmat and suited up but let it hang around his waist. He took a pair of binoculars and his camera with him to his car. Dr Creed followed him.

They drove in silence to the entrance to Harper Lake track. Wilbur noted the broken branches. He put on the suit fully adjusted the visor and Dr Creed zipped him in to seal it off. Dr Creed did the same and Wilbur made sure he was secured. They walked down through the trees it was eerily quiet except for the sound of his breathing through the regulator.

The valve made a popping sound as he sucked air in. As they neared the lake Wilbur spotted Jimmy's truck then a bit further in, he saw the figure sitting with his back against the tyre wall. He tried to shout but his voice was muffled by the heavy suit and condensation was dripping down his shirt. He raised the binoculars to the visor as best he could and focussed. He lowered them as if in doubt and returned them to see that it was no illusion.

All that was left of Jimmy were a mass of bones. He had been picked clean. Wilbur felt a salty tear start to run from his left eye down his cheek.

The guilty feeling surfaced as he had told him to come here. Jimmy died doing his sworn duty. Wilbur then scanned the area looking for Hepworth. But it didn't take long to find him. He was still holding on to the passenger side door handle in a rictus that suggested trying to enter the safety of the vehicles cab. All to no avail.

Elmer was watching the grass for any signs of movement. His breathing was laboured and nervously getting faster. The grass moved noticeably now and parted to reveal a Chigger much larger than the one in the Sheriff's office it plodded stolidly onward toward the scientist. "Holy shit that is one big bastard of a Chigger!" he said into the helmet.

Wilbur looked round for Elmer and saw him frozen to the spot. Then he saw why. He signalled to Elmer that they should go. Moving as fast as the suits would allow, they ran. Returning to the Dodge they jumped in making sure the windows and vents were securely shut before easing off the hooded part of their suits. They both started to talk at once, both said the same "Did you see the size of that fucker?" One of them chose to say bastard instead, so it was known as a fuckerbastard.

"If this wasn't such a dangerous business I would laugh at that statement. But this is no laughing matter." Said Wilbur. Elmer spoke quickly. "Do you realise that in a little over six hours there has been an almost doubling in size. I hope there aren't too many more of them."

Wilbur was too deep in thought to reply.

Then he said, "I saw Jimmy and Hepworth – picked clean, it was horrible."

6

Wilbur started the car and spun his wheels in the dust. Must calm down he thought and took his foot off the gas. At last, they gripped the path, and he reversed out onto the main highway.
He jumped out, grabbing some yellow tape and tied it across the track as quickly as he could before jumping back in the car, he gave a last look at his handiwork and sped off back to his office.

As they arrived, they were met by a smartly turned out young fresh-faced Captain in the National Guard. Wilbur extended a hand, but the Captain saluted him then extended his.

"Captain James Spencer sir! I would say pleased to meet you in normal circumstances, but this isn't normal is it?"

"You are right young man! Elmer and I have been out to the Lake to reconnoitre the area to see what we are up against. Come into the office and I will show you something that will knock ya socks off."

All three stood round the giant Chigger studying it. Wilbur broke the silence. "Son, this here is only a small one compared to the one we almost made contact with out at the lakeside, man, that was motherfucking huge er, pardon my language, in circumstances like this I tend to use such terminology."

Elmer Creed laughed nervously. "Yea I was petrified when that one come at me from out of the long grass. They are growing at a helluva rate!"

"I see, so they are growing you say. At what rate do you estimate Dr?"

"Hmm, well if it continues at the present pace, growth probably will be a couple of feet long after six hours or so. Plus, we don't know how many there are altogether!" He continued, "Not only that but they are moving out from the grassland onto farmland seeking out livestock. A farmer named Brown brought this one in. He said he lives a mile away from the central infestation. Sheriff, we need to evacuate the people who live near there right away. It won't be just livestock think of the fate of your Deputy?"

Wilbur looked up. "Dammit! I almost forgot about them and Brown!" He banged his fist on the desk, "Those Chiggers are gonna pay for killing my deputy!"

"Right give me a minute and I can organise an evac of the area and establish some kind of perimeter, we have to contain these things, before they get much bigger and harder to handle!" Capt. Spencer said before he headed out to his Jeep and spoke quickly to his radio operator "Get me HQ on the radio."

"HQ, Capt. James Spencer here. We have an extreme emergency Code Red, I repeat Code Red. Need all personnel in the area to RP Calico County Sheriff office asap and require all the flamethrowers we have, I repeat flamethrowers all we have! Out." He handed the radio back. Wilbur had come outside to see the Captain taking charge. "Son, I hope you don't mind me calling you that? But there are at least five families out there that need to be brought into town for their protection! I have the names and addresses right here. Would you get them? Appreciate it." He handed over the list. It was handed to the radio operator in turn, and he made the call to HQ.

Within minutes wagons and helicopters were dispatched to the farms listed.

7

Dan Brown heard his cattle crying out in an unearthly way. It started with one then more added to the sound, it tore at his heart. Because Dan had put all he had into building up his dairy herd. Now it seemed as though he will be ruined because of an oversized bug. He ran to the barn and swung open the door.

The cattle were rubbing frantically at the walls of their pen trying to rid themselves of the large biting, itching insects but more jumped on their backs fastening their fangs deep into the helpless animals' flesh, the sucking noise was horrendous. Dan could only stand and watch the carnage before him.

Soon all was silent the voracious feeding stopped, and the insects dropped off to lie limp on the floor. He ran to get the weed burner, and, in a frenzy, he lit up every one of the grossly fattened creatures that lay there. He moved here and there seeking them out. Finally done, he heaved a sigh of relief, sat on an upturned bucket and wiped the sweat from his brow.

From a hole in the roof a set of eyes regarded him closely. It smelt blood and suddenly dropped on him. This one was two feet long, the sheer weight dropping down onto him knocked the breath out of him and he hit the floor hard, Dan felt the fangs dig deep into his neck where it injected an enzyme that liquified his tissue quickly allowing the chigger to siphon off his blood. He started to drift into unconsciousness before he died. The Chigger drained him completely. Dan like Jimmy and Hepworth became nothing more than a husk with clothes.

It stayed in position for some time, lethargic due to its huge feed but somehow it knew that it would be producing more offspring to replace those that had been killed today. Gradually, it moved its limbs and slowly climbed back to its vantage point in the roof.

Vera Brown had heard the commotion created by the cattle but wondered where Dan had gone and strangely the cattle had become silent.

She walked over to the barn where the door was banging back and forth in the breeze. "Damn it Dan why don't you close these doors after you?" She fumed. As she was closing the door something caught her eye. It was flat on the floor and at first she thought, why had Dan made a scarecrow? We don't have any crops. Her hand flew to her mouth to cover a scream as she recognised the corpse of her husband. She closed the door hard and bolted it. The Chigger watched her, still very lethargic from feeding.

Vera ran as fast as she could to the house and slammed the door shut, locked and bolted every window and when satisfied, she phoned the Sheriff. She held the phone so tightly her knuckles were turning white. She cast glances over her shoulders both left and right to see if there was any clue as to the means of how her husband was killed, but nothing moved or stirred everywhere she looked.

"Sheriff's office – Maisie speaking how can I help you?"
"Maisie! Thank God you answered. I need the Sheriff quickly!" The words just tumbled out of her mouth.
"Who is this please? I cannot hear what you are saying. Please speak slowly and clearly, you sound very stressed so take a deep breath calm yourself and let me know what you require?"

"Maisie! It's me Vera Brown from out near Harper Mill just south of Breenville. I need to talk to the Sheriff, its Dan my husband. He… he is dead, and I don't know what killed him. So please can I talk to the Sheriff now?"

"Vera, I am sorry, but Sheriff Deeds is out of the office with Dr Creed, and I don't know when he will be back. However, I can call him on the radio to see if he is near your place or if he can get there? Will that do?" Maisie spoke pausing for a moment as she heard sobs from the other end of the line "Vera? Vera are you alright dear?"

"Yes! Yes, that will have to do but please hurry I am so scared out here." Vera sniffed.

Maisie grabbed the radio and called Wilbur straightaway "Sheriff come in Sheriff can you hear me. WILBUR!! Pick up your damn radio and answer me." She shouted, thinking that Wilbur was just ignoring her, which for the most part he did just to wind her up. However, Wilbur was actually headed in the direction of the Brown's farm as it had been the first point of contact for the infestation. The radio had been silent since the route to the farm had been taken and on a bend in the road it suddenly crackled into life. Maisie's staccato voice boomed into the air. "WILBUR! Pick up your damn radio and answer me?"

Wilbur swerved at the screech.

"Sweet Mother of Jesus, Maisie, I almost lost my car! Whatdya want honey?"

"Vera Brown just called, she was in a helluva state, something or somebody killed her husband, she sounded terrified on the telephone just now! Where are you?"

"Actually, we are headed there right now maybe bout ten minutes away now! Leave it with me I'll get back to yuh soon as ah find out the problem ok?" He put the radio back in the cradle. Wilbur had a cold feeling running up and down his spine but didn't want to panic Maisie. He turned to his passenger, "Elmer! I got a nasty feeling bout this! Dan Brown is dead. I think those darn Chiggers got to him. Vera, his wife, is holed up in their home." Elmer just nodded quietly.

8

Wilbur pulled up at the Brown farmhouse.
He looked through the dusty windshield, saw that it was clear and made a dash for the door. He knocked rapidly and shouted for Vera.
She looked cautiously out from a shaking curtain and swiftly opened the door. "Sheriff thank God you have come. Dan is in the barn! Well, his clothes are, but he is just a skeleton inside them. I don't know what happened to him but there is a strange smell of stale blood in there and I didn't want to hang around to find out what it was. I am still shaking like a darn leaf!" she sobbed.

    Wilbur decided to come clean about the events that brought them here. "Chiggers about six feet across Vera! That is the problem. Someone messed about with chemicals and dumped them in the lake, and this is what we get! Something out of a horror movie only this time it's for real! Vera you better come with us, and we can call out the guard to deal with this. Bring Dan's gun and plenty of ammunition!

Vera had already grabbed a Winchester from the pegs above the fireplace and managed to find all four boxes that Dan had put in his desk drawer. She stuffed them hastily into her apron pocket and with the rifle tucked under her arm she and Wilbur raced for the parked car, hauled the doors open and both jumped in slamming them shut behind them. They were inside for a few short moments when there was a bang and a large dent appeared in the roof. A chigger had leaped onto the roof and was trying to open the metal by raking its mandibles across the top. Fortunately, it was unable to gain access.

Vera pointed the rifle upward and pulled the trigger. A deafening roar filled the vehicle as the gun went off and a small hole appeared in the roof. After a few seconds a drop of blood fell through the hole to land on her shoulder, followed by a scrabbling sound and the chigger slid down over windshield and off the hood to land in the dust just in front of them.

Vera screamed but it was not a fearful scream it was rather a scream of vengeance, "That's for my Dan you bastard stink bug!" She cranked the lever and loaded up another round ready for the next encounter.

Wilbur started the engine and gunned it. The wheels stirred up the dust and threw off some smoke as he reversed away from the body of the chigger. He stopped suddenly when an obstruction presented at his rear. Another bug had managed to grab his rear wheel and was trying to puncture the tire with a claw. More chiggers were arranging themselves into a circle waiting for their opportunity to attack.

He selected first gear and gunned it again, spinning the wheel and aimed for a gap between two chiggers. The chigger that had grabbed the wheel so hard found it had an empty claw when the wheel was suddenly torn from its grasp by the sudden forward momentum caused by the car surging forward and hitting the two blocking the way, their heads being so close that they shattered on contact with the heavy vehicle. The sudden impact was strong enough to turn their bodies in unison. Once free the open road beckoned.

Grabbing at his radio, he called Gina, "Get hold of that Captain of the National Guard and get them out here to Brown's Farm asap." He threw the radio to Elmer to put it back, muttering to himself as he placed it in the cradle, "I'm so glad I stayed in the car back there."

Wilbur's hand shook as he wrestled with the wheel trying to keep it going straight on the twisting farm track back to town.   At last, the town loomed into view and the sight of some National Guard trucks seemed to calm him down.
The car rolled to a tire flopping stop in front of the Sheriff's office the last of its air wheezing out like the last breath of dying man.
    "That was fucking too damn close! Ooh, sorry Vera for my language." Suddenly, remembering her presence.
"Oh! Don't worry on my account Sheriff I agree it was very fucking close!"
    They burst out laughing as Vera said it. Their nervousness and adrenaline, slowly coming down to a more normal level.

    Wilbur had to shoulder his door to get out, the impact of hitting chiggers at speed had not been without some consequences. His wing mirror dangled loosely, the hood peeled back on one corner and a fold in the middle caused it to look like a strange fish like mouth. Similar indentations appeared on the passenger side as well as a large gash along the rear passenger door.

The Sheriff breathed a sigh of relief, at least he and his passengers were safe for the moment.
He hitched up his britches using his gun belt and strode inside his station. Walked calmly to his desk and slid out the top drawer. It was only as he removed a brass tagged key ring from under a pile of papers, he noticed his now trembling hands. Up until then he looked cool and calm and acted how a Sheriff should act.

Stifling the urge to sob he turned to the metal cabinet on his right and inserted the key, he swung the metal door back from his prized collection of guns and ammunition. A solid chain ran through the guards of the rifles and shotguns keeping them held securely to the cabinet wall where it ended in a strong padlock. Fumbling at the fob he found the other key on the ring and opened it, removing the chain hastily. It rattled through leaving the weapons exposed.

He made his selection, favouring a pump action shotgun and a Glock automatic he found in the metal drawer along with a few boxes of shells and cartridges, he quickly stuffed them in his jacket pocket.
He also checked the weapons several times as if unsure and loaded them up ready for use. Finally, satisfied, he flicked on their safeties.

9

Wilbur stood on the top step and looked forlorn at the state of his car. "Damn she won't hold together much more now!" he muttered sadly. His eyes scanned the town square for something a bit more substantial he could commandeer.

Just as Wilbur had spotted the large black truck in the alley belonging to the butcher Harvey Baines, an army truck pulled up and three very smartly dressed soldiers jumped out. They saw the Sheriff and as one they saluted him.

"No need to salute me boys! Well I'll be a horny toad it's the terrible trio!!" He exclaimed.

Chet stepped forward and shook his hand the others followed, "We wanted to thank you for setting us straight Sheriff! Thanks to you we have passed our exams, and you are looking at Sergeant Chet Watkins, Specialist Carl Spender and Technician Will Benton."

"Well now son, I already know how you boys got on. Let you into a little secret, Colonel James D. Waite your commanding officer is an old war buddy of mine. I asked him to keep a watch on you all and to provide regular reports. You were all astounding! I knew you could do it and given the right conditions, but you did it. You worked hard. Anyway, we have ourselves a bit of a problem here in Calico and y'all have a hand in helping along with your Guard buddies." The Sheriff stopped and shook their hands again.

Turning, he called out "Good Luck guys!" Wilbur raced to the truck.

Harvey was about to get in and noticed the Sheriff waving at him, "What's up Sheriff?"
"Gonna need your pickup Harvey!"
"Shit! What the heck for?"
"Oh, er, for official business Harvey, yep can't tell ya cos ya not a deputy!" Wilbur shot a quick wink at Vera who had made her way over to the pair.

Harvey was puzzled but never questioned why Vera, a civilian, was there too.

He solemnly handed over his keys to his 1985 Ford Bronco which had become a prized possession of his in the few weeks he had owned it.

10

Zebediah Barstow was a dour Scot who had emigrated some 30 years previous, he had two sons by his first wife Hannah who had succumbed to cancer shortly after the birth of their second child and Zebediah was left with two boys to rear. He often worked them long and hard into the night, his heart turned inward through grief. Yet both boys knew his burden was heavy and would never let it show on their faces or mention their mother as they calmly worked on for their father's sake.

Gradually their ranch grew in size and revenue. Their stock handpicked for their survival under the harshest conditions. Despite his gruff exterior anyone who had dealings with Old Zeb as he was affectionately known (although this was not said to his face) knew he was a fair and honest dealer.

Now Zeb and his boys had their ranch some ten miles out of town and their stock grazed freely on the scrub six miles from Harper Lake. He never liked putting up fences around his stock, merely relying on the honesty of his neighbours returning them whenever they spotted his brand.

    Due to this Dan and Vera quite often had to repair their fences when Zeb's cattle took to roaming, Dan would have to rope the odd steer and drag it back onto Zeb's land. Then he would see one of the boys, most likely it would be Henry the oldest Barstow looking for it and deliver it with the message, "Tell that old Pa of yours if it comes back, we gonna be eating prime steak! I ain't a nursemaid nor one of your hands Henry Barstow!"

Henry always laughed and shooed the steer back to the herd.

***

Henry heard the scream of a steer and rode off the general direction of the sound. It made him shiver. His horse felt jumpy underneath him and he knew that something must have seriously affected him because he had raised Buck from a colt and nothing would faze him, neither heat nor cold. His head would just lower, and he would take it all in his stride.

    Henry's blood ran cold when he spotted the steer and the Chigger that was creating the ghastly scream. He leaped out of the saddle, took out his Colt .45 and fired at the monster insect. A slug hit it between the eyes with a squelch and the recoil toppled it from its squirming victim. The steer's knees buckled under it as the weight left it's back, but it was too late it had lost too much of its precious life-giving fluid. The Chigger lay on its back legs flailing unable to regain its equilibrium. Turning to Buck who had stood so still, he pulled his Winchester from the leather case that hung on the animal's rump and pumped three rounds into its stinking carcass then swung up into the saddle and grabbed the reins tightly before he swung the horse around and high tailed it back to the ranch house.

    Henry dismounted before Buck had time to stop and ran up the wooden steps at full pelt. He flung the door wide and gasped out his experience with the Chigger. Zeb looked at him as if he was drunk and grunted.
    Edward the younger Barstow tried to calm his brother's apparent ramblings and handed him a glass of rye whiskey. A quick swig and Henry coughed as the liquor worked its way down to his innards. "Am telling ya Pa it was a monster insect an it was eating a steer sitting all pretty as you like up on its back!" Zeb looked coldly at Henry, "You been making moonshine boy?"

"No sir I swear on our Momma's grave I saw it an I shot the bastard too"

"Don't you cuss using Momma boy! I kin still give you a whuppin!"

"Pa, Pa, Henry don't lie. If he killed a monster insect, then he killed it?" Said Edward.

"If ya don't' believe me get in the wagon an I will take you out there to it! Wanna know sumthin funny? Dan Brown was nowhere to be seen and he used to bring that old steer back."

"Ok Henry, get the wagon hitched up for us." Zeb pulled himself painfully up from his armchair and headed to the barn, all following behind.

They were silent as they hitched up the wagon, assisted him into the seat and swung themselves up beside him. Henry grabbed the reins, and they rode off to see the monster.

The horses started to jump from side to side threatening to dislodge them, their nostrils flared, and they whinnied with fear. Zeb conceded that there was indeed an air of menace in the atmosphere. They tethered their team to a nearby tree and walked gingerly over to the body of the Chigger. Zeb emitted a loud, "Holee Shit that is one helluva bug?
Zeb had to agree with his boy.
"Henry ya certainly didn't lie son, I'm sorry!"

Edward looked around nervously.
Henry spotted his edginess, "Cat got ya tongue Eddie?"
"Well, if that was the only one, I would be fine, but I got a nasty feeling there may be more, so I am jest waiting?"
Henry drew his gun and looked nervously around. "Ok, let's get the hell away from here!"

They scurried back to the tethered team just in time to hear a branch cracking and a heavy crashing heading their way. The team both reared in reply and almost cracked open Henry's skull as they both brought their hooves within inches of him. They jumped up on the wagon, Henry had already given them their head and they flew off in a cloud of dust just as another Chigger lurched through the bushes. Zebediah let out a huge sigh of relief.
Edward was nervously looking back over his shoulder as if the very devil were chasing them.

Henry steered the wagon back to the ranch. Suddenly the air was filled with a swirling choking dust storm and a loud whooshing sound could be heard above them.
A helicopter slowly landed a few feet away from them its rotors slowly winding down with a whine and a dozen soldiers emerged from within.

A tall blonde Captain ran up to the group. "Mr Barstow?" He asked.
"Yessir! What kin ah do fer ya?" Replied Zeb.
"We need you and your boys to grab some stuff and we are going to take you into town."
"What about my stock?"
"Sorry sir but you are in danger being here!"
"I ain't leaving, I have seen those thing's, and I am not letting them get the rest of ma beef ya unnerstand?" Zeb planted his feet firmly and placed his hands defiantly on his hips.
"But sir we have a lot more fire power than you currently have, and we would stand a better chance of getting rid of them."
"Paw, the Captain is right, what kin we do with a couple of rifles, an old shotgun and Grand pappy's old Remington?" Said Henry.

Zeb felt small and weak in the face of this new menace. He had met every challenge life had thrown and met them head on. He knew deep down they were right. His shoulders dropped and he just shrugged. Turning he walked up the porch steps and went inside closely followed by his sons.
They emerged with some clothes wrapped in bedding rolls and mounted the wagon and horses.
"We can fly you into town?"
"No thanks! We kin get there ourselves!"

"Be careful then, keep a sharp lookout for the chiggers!" He turned to the squad and barked out his orders, "Squad break off into your groups and search the area. Report any activity and burn them up where you can!"

"YESSIR!" Answering in unison with a salute.

11

Each group took a different route and spread out using the farmhouse as a central point.
They examined every building and outhouse for evidence of insect habitation. Each area designated and voiced clear over the airwaves. So far so good they all thought. As they spread their search the groups would get further away from each other. The men became very nervous and jumped at every sound.

    In the northern quadrant a group of soldiers heard the screaming cry of a cow. They looked fearfully at each other and cautiously headed toward the unearthly sound. As they came into a clearing, they saw three large chiggers latching onto a cow and her calf. The animal was trying to stamp on the chigger that had her baby. It was firmly locked onto its young neck. It could not utter a sound and it fell to the ground like a deflated balloon.

There was a chigger on each side of the cow, and they watched in horror as her footsteps faltered and then she too succumbed to their voracious appetites. As they dropped off to lie semi-comatose. A soldier opened fire with his gun set on automatic, it bucked in his hands sending blood and guts spinning into the air. Another opened up his flamethrower to incinerate the carcasses into ash.

The last soldier heard a sound behind him, and he turned to find not one but four chiggers approaching. He trembled at the thought that they had got behind them without him seeing them. However, releasing his safety he managed to fire in quick succession and managed to drop them. The flamethrower was put into use again and the flames rose quickly.

"Northern quadrant has infestation! Over!" the radio operator reported as more chiggers appeared in the grass.

The flame operative sprayed a wide area in front of them to provide a protective wall against the oncoming invasion. It stopped them for a short time long enough for the other groups to assemble in support.

They held their fire observing the actions of the chiggers. Some moved forward but stopped as they felt the heat. Others appeared to be pushing them up to the point where they died and then calmly walked over the charred corpses of their comrades. On they marched until more flames and bullets halted their progress.

The soldier suddenly found that his flame was sputtering and coughing until no inflammable material could be seen from the red-hot end.
Onward they marched on relentlessly. Intuitively, they pushed on toward the small group of men. Standing in shocked silence until one soldier decided he could not stand it any longer and let fly a volley of bullets from his automatic. This action signalled the others to open fire in the forlorn hope that these creatures would either turn aside or stop their onslaught. Unfortunately, the sound of gunfire died down as quickly as it had started.

The volley did not stop the relentless death march of the chiggers. They overran the group's position and fell upon them voraciously, injecting and chewing the hapless men into a bloody mess. Their screams joined with the farm animals in a never-ending cacophony of pain and agonising death.

Chet and the team arrived in time to see the carnage the chiggers had caused to their comrades and their subsequent retreat to digest their meal.

"Blast these bastards to hell!" Chet shouted.

A rain of liquid fire fell on the fleeing chiggers, while a hail of bullets cut the clambering insects down. The overall stench of burning flesh permeated the air, bringing tears to the eyes and a raw, hacking cough. "Cease fire!" Chet coughed as the taste of acidic bile came into his mouth. He pulled his canteen and drank deeply. The water soothed his burning throat momentarily. He swilled it around and spat some onto the sandy soil at his feet. "Hot damn, these suckers take some killing!" He said to no one in particular.

"Hey Sarge! I sure fried them really good, didn't I?"

"Ya sure did Carl! But don't git carried away, there are more of them than there are of us!"

"And they are smart too!" Will added, "Sarge? How big do ya reckon they are now because I heard they were about five feet across?"

"Well! By my reckoning they must be about nearer ten now! Each time they feed they grow a bit more. Pretty soon they will just over run our positions so keep on the lookout for any activity?"

"Right, better call in our position and give them a sit rep?" Will spoke as he twisted the dials for a response to his call.

All he could hear was an ominous crackling in his headset. He tried several frequencies, but nothing came through. His face registered some concern as he turned to Chet to report his findings. Chet realised that they were now operating on their own. He suddenly held up his hand, "Gunfire! Some way off! Ok guys, time we head out in that direction." He said pointing south-east, "Eyes peeled and careful walking boys, silent mode too, unless you encounter the bugs."

12

Wilbur gunned the engine of the Bronco and almost threw it into gear. Harvey could only watch with a pained expression as his pride and joy was driven away. He hoped rather forlornly that Wilbur would bring it back in one piece, shrugged his shoulders and went inside.

Wilbur called the scientist.

"What progress you got?"

Elmer Creed looked down at his shoes and cleared his throat, "Sorry Wilbur it's a dead end. The formula we made to destroy the Chiggers has not had the desired effect. It's too weak."

"That was not the news I wanted to hear today Elmer! Keep at it then see if you can come up with something stronger and more effective."

"We, that is Vera, and I are heading out aways to some more farms to try an get a report on the Chiggers movements!"

"Take care Sheriff they will be about 12 feet long by now. They had time to grow since their last feeding frenzy?"

***

Chet and his group met up with two more teams as they worked their way toward the transport that waited at their RP. They were becoming more and more nervous and would become startled at every crack of twig underfoot. But then they had every right to be nervous as several chiggers lay in wait behind a small pile of rocks just off the beaten path.

Corporal Dickens had just turned to the group to signal when a sudden dark shadow fell across him. Chet shouted just in time to see him duck behind a fallen log as a chigger dropped with a thud onto an empty space. A space that should have held one Corporal Dickens.

A blaze of gunfire and liquid fire poured onto the insect and once more the acrid stench of frying flesh filled their lungs. They had no time to celebrate as two more joined the fray.

Jack Dickens tripped over a root as the larger of two chiggers made a lunge for the group. He tucked and rolled as best as he could but on regaining his footing discovered that his guard had bent and made the trigger inoperable.

His flamethrower was effectively useless. More or less thinking on his feet, he undid his harness and flung the tank of gasoline at the approaching chigger's head, shouting to the team "Fire at the tank boys!"

A burst of machine gun fire caught the flying tank exploding it with a roar, flaming liquid coating both chiggers and brought them down. The explosion threw them all to the floor, while flaming embers and pieces of damaged trees flew in all directions.

***

Wilbur and Vera were cruising along nervously looking from side to side in case the chiggers were in their vicinity. The engine almost purred. Wilbur deep in thought suddenly heard Vera scream.

"What?" he gasped.
"Look! Over there! I heard an explosion and saw a huge column of smoke. The forest is on fire!"
"I saw a group of soldiers running through the trees and there were chiggers moving after them!"

The ragged assembly of soldiers had emerged onto the highway.
Wilbur caught up with them and skidded to a halt before he wound his window down. "Get in boys and make it snappy those chiggers will be here soon!" Their gear was stowed in the back, and they squeezed onto the flat bed just as the chiggers reached the forest edge. Wilbur gunned the engine and the rear wheels started smoking and squealing in protest before they finally took a grip on the asphalt road and sped off leaving them behind.
"Lucky we happened along boys?" he shouted over the purr of the engine.
"Yea any later and we would be insect food!" one of the soldiers replied.
"Where are you headed Sheriff?" Chet interjected.
"Well we were about to check out the Anderson ranch bout 10 miles out! You?"
"Heading to our pickup point for supplies and report in. Let's see, on my map it is about 6 or 7 miles away"
"Well I can drop you boys near to your base? If that is okay?"
"Sure, is thanks. Saved us a hike!" Chet laughed.

Sometime later Wilbur pulled up brakes squealing. Chet and the other men vaulted out of their cramped space and stretched, rubbing their legs to restore their circulation. Wilbur waved them off as they headed to the base. He eased off the handbrake and accelerated away hoping that he could get this infestation under control, and also hoping that the Anderson ranch was still intact. He thought, what a shitstorm this has turned out to be.

Unfortunately, his thought was spoken out loud. Vera laughed and agreed.
Wilbur looked at her in astonishment. "Jeez, did I say that out loud?" He muttered.
"Sure, did you old coot! But you are entitled to your opinion and for once I agree with you. A right shitstorm indeed!"
They both laughed and felt the tension ease a little as they pulled up in front of Mike Anderson's ranch.
It was eerily quiet.

Wilbur took his shotgun from a mount in the pickup truck. He cocked it and loaded a shell into the breach then cautiously moved toward the house.
His footfall was both quiet and steady, not wishing to come upon a chigger unawares. Suddenly the front door opened, barely a crack but enough to see a long barrel poking out and a crackling wheezy voice demanding! "Who is there? Show yersel or I swear I'll drill ya full o'lead!"

"Mike it's me Wilbur – put that ole peashooter down afore ya hurt yourself!"

"Advance and be recognised!"

"Mike ya ain't in the military now ya old coot! Put yer spectacles on and look it's me!"

"Sorry Sheriff goin a might deef these days!"

"Mike – have you seen anything weird up here lately?"

"Well, I saw sasquatch walking past the barn, but I thought it wuz the moonshine I had." Mike laughed and coughed.

Wilbur stared hard at him.

Mike gave a nervous laugh and realised that Wilbur was being deadly serious.

"Damn it Mike, this is for real, if one of these bastard giant chiggers had seen you or gotten wind of you, I wouldn't be standing here on your porch jawing with ya!"

Vera looked up at the sky as the sound of flapping wings echoed through the air and watched as a flock of birds rose and fell, wheeling through the air.

They had been disturbed quite badly apparently as they desperately tried to fly away from the area. Wilbur broke off his conversation with Old Mike to observe their behaviour. He surmised it was the insects barging their way through the undergrowth that had set them into a frenzy.

If only humans were blessed with wings, then maybe they too could get away from these loathsome creatures he thought.

"Ya say these here chiggers are more than 16 feet long. An how high? Over 6 feet! Holee shit! "Whutcha gonna do about em Sheriff?" Mike peered into Wilbur's face trying to gauge his reaction through his rheumy eyes.

"Well, we have the National Guard boys helping but might have to call in the US Marines?" Wilbur held his thoughts in check, he knew deep down that this situation was getting out of hand. He didn't really know what he was going to do.

He just hoped and prayed that it would come to an end and offered up a short prayer – and please God make it soon.

13

They grabbed some of Mike's belongings and slung them in the back seat. As he followed, Wilbur slammed the door as quickly as he could hitting Mike in the process, knocking him sideways onto the seat. Mike just lay there stunned for a moment. Righting himself he let loose with a volley of the rudest, crudest words to ever emerge from an old man.

Wilbur just looked at him in the rear-view mirror and burst out laughing. Mike stopped, realising that there was a lady inside the vehicle. His face went bright red, and he mumbled an apology. Vera just turned and fixed him with a stare that gave the impression that she would not stand for such behaviour.

Then she too dissolved into fits of laughter.

Mike was too embarrassed to look her in the eye.
"Mike, it was an accident and we needed to get away in case that insect came back on us. Ya'll understand now?"
"Yea, but that door hit me right in the ass! It sure made me see stars. My head hit my goddamn gun. Let's go then, cuz times awastin!"

Wilbur started the engine and drove off.

***

Dr Creed sat at his desk checking the figures of the latest test batch. He almost jumped for joy. The mixture was the closest he had seen at last it looked like they had something to use against the infestation. The only thing now was to test it out in the field. His heart was racing, and he felt the surge of adrenaline coursing through him now. He remembered his last encounter and suddenly became fearful. He picked up the telephone and spoke to the switchboard. "Gina! Get me the Sheriff's office, this is vital information, please hurry!"
Gina put down her newly filled coffee cup and pulled on a wire and re-routed it to a socket on her board and heard the click as it made a connection.

"Sheriff's office, Maisie Watkins here how can I help you?"

"Hi, this is Sheraton Chemicals on behalf of Dr Elmer Creed, he would like to talk to the Sheriff it's urgent!"
"Sorry, but Sheriff is out on business, can I take a message?" Maisie replied, as she reached for her note pad.
"No, is there some way you can get him on the radio and tell him to contact Dr Creed as soon as he can!"
"Well honey, I can sure try for you, give me a few minutes." Maisie told the receptionist as she turned to the radio operator that had been assigned to the office and asked him to put a call out to Sheriff Deeds.
After a few agonising minutes there was a confirmation that Wilbur had replied. "Well honey, we have contacted Sheriff Deeds, he is on his way back to the office right now!'
Gina paused for a moment to pass on the message Dr Creed.
"Ok, tell him I will meet him there as soon as I can?." Dr Creed replied, the stress in his voice clearly audible. Elmer could only imagine what was happening further out from the town. He sincerely hoped that his formula was the right one to end the nightmare the country was about to face.

14

Colonel Waites face was ashen as he listened to the daily reports. Many of his finest young men were being killed by bugs. Not war or battles just huge bugs. He decided that it was time to contact the President and outline the case for declaring a National Emergency. He picked up the telephone and called his superior in the Pentagon. A hurried conversation and it was transmitted further up the chain of Command until it reached the ears of the President.

***

Gathering his advisors around him the President looked out on a sea of anxious faces and called for suggestions. Someone wanted to quarantine the town and surrounding areas. Another suggested martial law and to keep the locals unaware of the true nature of the problem. Another argued that it was a bit late for that as the locals were being transported out of the danger zone as they were speaking. Someone suggested that they cordon off the area as best they could and send in a warhead to blow them up. The President looked shocked at this proposal and flatly refused to sanction such a remedy. However, he suggested the troops be deployed quickly to the area to help the National Guard in their defence of the town and the inhabitants.

****

    Elmer arrived at the Sheriff's office clutching a sheaf of papers. Wilbur had arrived an hour later greedily swallowing a hot cup of coffee, nearly removing the lining of his throat in the process. He coughed.
    "Okay Elmer, what is the goddamn rush? Wilbur sat down hard in his chair facing Dr Creed. "It is this formula we have been working on since I got back to the lab. I have been working to get something to stop their progression. This one is one hundred thirty-eight. My guys caught a couple of the smaller buggers, you know those ones around 6ft long. I don't know if it will work on anything larger?"

Wilbur looked at Elmer and felt sorry for the dishevelled little scientist. He looked like he had not slept for some time.

"I also suggest we ignite Harper's Mill pond!" Elmer declared.

Wilbur was about to take another sip from his cup and almost dropped it. "I thought you said it would be a huge explosion once it went up?"

"Well, everyone has been evacuated and we can burn every piece of vegetation around for about a mile. Create some firebreaks and that should stop them getting at more chemicals. We spray our formula for another mile or so out and monitor the area"

"Well, it sounds like a reasonable plan to me, but we have to convince those guys in charge because it has now moved up to a National Emergency and I believe the President has his ear to the ground now?"

15

Capt. Spencer was informed of the plan, and he sent it winging its way up the chain for their approval. Col. Waite gave it the go ahead but even he had to wait while it was scrutinised further. Finally, it arrived back onto Col. Waite's desk, and he noticed the President's seal and signature.

The telephone never stopped it's incessant ringing as he co-ordinated the operations.

The locals were told to stay in their homes and to keep away from all windows. Not to go outside for any reason while manoeuvres were being carried out. A media block was placed on the town. But a short statement to the effect that this was an exercise of National Importance that was taking place was issued. Then radio and television silence were imposed. Some locals were curious and tried to step out of their homes but were made to turn back thanks to a few well-placed soldiers, who were heavily armed.

The engineers were sent to bulldoze an area around the Mill and just beyond the tree line. Huge piles of earth pushed aside to create a large gap soon began to appear. Tankers with the formula awaited at Sheraton Chemicals for their part in the show.

Col. Waite checked his watch and synchronised it with his Commanders. "In five gentlemen, four, three, two, one! At 01.00 fire your incendiaries into Harper's Pond. After ignition send three into surrounding area and monitor blaze! Now go take up your positions."

Everyone scrambled into their jeeps and set off. Each Commander radioed back to confirm they were in place. As their watches slowly revolved to 01.00 the order for incendiary rockets rang out. A collection of whooshes signified that they had been launched. The barrage hurtled into the air like a series of hornets and as they descended into the Pond there appeared a blueish green flame on the surface momentarily accompanied by an ear-splitting bang as the gaseous leakage ignited in full fury. A further series of rockets took to the air to fall into the trees and bushes surrounding the Pond. Sadly, the Old Mill took a direct hit and burst into flames. The conflagration lasted for a good 24 hours.

The prepared gap held the flames in check as predicted. Local fire tenders fastened pumps to the tankers and sprayed the areas outlined in the plan. Jets of formula were aimed at the surviving vegetation and drenched. Within a few minutes chiggers of all sizes burst out of the undergrowth. Slowly they turned brown and stopped moving.

Elmer ran around collecting samples of the deceased blood sucking insects. Choosing a good selection of sizes, he put each one in a jar and sealed it.

Chet and his guys were recalled to HQ outside of the strike zone. Capt. Spencer reassigned them to a platoon of battle-hardened Marines who instantly took a dislike to them. Although their comments were scornful and brutal, they just kept quiet. They knew what they were up against while these guys had not even seen this enemy neither before nor since. Fighting in jungles and deserts against similarly armed forces were one thing, but gigantic insects were quite another. Still Chet and his trustworthy team had an opportunity to get some well-earned rest and some chow. They stood in line with their army issue trays and held them out to receive the portion from the poised ladles of the cooks. Then as one turned to the tables set out in the mess tent that had so conveniently been set up for them.

Will turned to Chet and whispered, "Those assholes are going to be crying for their Momma when they see the bugs!" He chuckled quietly.

Carl was busy ramming forkfuls of mash into his mouth like it was his last meal.

"Slow down Carl before you choke" Chet jibed.

"Well, who knows when we gonna get another hot meal? C'mon Sarge you know I'm right!"

Chet reluctantly had to agree with Carl's observations. "I have been thinking about these bugs. We are the ones chasing the bastards and getting picked off by them!"

Carl and Will's curiosities were piqued, and both men turned facing Chet's direction. Both started to talk at once. "What is your plan then Sarge?"

"Ok, remember when we took a ride out to Red Butte that summer? When we went looking for Indian artefacts?"

"What about it?" Carl spoke, through a mouthful of meatloaf and mash.

"There was a natural corral formed by those cliffs! If we get some steers in there, those bugs are gonna be just dyin' to get in there to them an believe me that is what they are gonna be doing. Dyin'! an as painful as I can make it for those suckers to avenge all of the National Guard that were killed by these things!"

"How do ya know we'll get all of them then?' Will asked.

"I need to get some intel on them as soon as I can! Plus, I have to convince the higher ups to accept my plan?" Chet finished his coffee and stood up. The others watched him leave. Striding purposefully through the doorway he thrust the makeshift door aside making it rebound closed behind him. He found the onsite comms tent and went in. Banks of flickering screens were being monitored by rows of technicians with headphones and microphones attached.

Chet tapped the nearest operator who slowly removed his headset "What is the latest on these bugs?"

"Well sarge they appear to be moving North and East now."

"Can you tell how many there are?" Chet asked as he bit his lip.

"Hard to say, those things are smart. They are using the cover of the trees. Keeping just outta sight of the choppers. Personally, I reckon maybe about a dozen on the move. But I am only guessing" He confided. "Are you asking in an official capacity sarge or unofficial?"

"Unofficial kid, quite unofficial and huh you aint seen me ok?" Chet placed his finger alongside his nose in reply. North, he thought good that ties in nicely with my plans for them before heading off to find Capt. Spencer for the next stage of his plan.

16

The good Captain was at his makeshift desk. Reading a sheaf of papers outlining the bugs movements. Chet stood to attention and saluted.
"What can I do for you Sergeant?"
"It is more what I can do for you sir!"
The Captain looked up quickly "Go on."
He walked over to a map that was pinned to an easel. It had the movements of the insects marked in red. It also listed areas that had overrun the squads that controlled the zone.
"Up here to the North there is a natural corral, it has only one way in and one way out." Chet started, his finger pointing out the landmark of Red Butte situated to the North of Calico County. "So, I reckon with a good supply of steers in there those blood suckers will

be itching to feed on some fresh meat. And we can have ourselves a good ole cookout of chigger ass, no offence sir?"

"None taken sergeant, kind of agree with you on that sentiment." Capt. Spencer replied as he looked down at the latest status update on the bugs which confirmed that they were indeed heading in a northerly direction. A further suggestion mentioned a possible search for more food. He looked up, "Are you sure that this plan will work?"

"Yessir, with the cooperation of the owners of the steers, we should be able to get the bugs before they even reach the cattle!"

"Right, leave it with me and I will get back to you? That will be all Sergeant!" He dismissed Chet with a salute. As Chet turned to head out he overheard Capt. Spencer on his telephone asking for his superior officer. Chet smiled to himself and hoped that Spencer would not claim this idea as his own.

A little while later Chet approached some of the ranchers to ask for their cooperation. Some voiced strong objections to the plan outlined but Chet managed to convince them that the government would recompense them for any cattle that were maimed or killed in the process. The objectors reluctantly agreed to his proposal. Admittedly, his fingers were crossed as he said it. He hoped that this would be the case from the circumstances in which they found themselves.

He would worry about it after the plan had been accepted. All that remained was to gather the herd of steers for the bait.

Chet had just reached the comms tent when the call came in that the plan had been approved by his superior officers. Command gave orders that as he had local knowledge he was to be in charge, and he could enlist any personnel to assist him in this task. He immediately signed up his friends and a couple of others who had worked on the outlying ranches.

Trey Fontaine, a twenty-seven-year-old rangy young man who had worked with cattle nearly all his life from early morning to late into the night before he eventually joined the National Guard didn't reckon he would be back in the saddle when he joined up. But talk reached him that Sergeant Chet Watkins was looking for experienced horsemen that knew the area and Trey presented himself to Chet.
"I have experience working around here Sarge! I kin ride too!"

"Ok, you will do, meet your new buddies this is Carl Spender and Will Benton." He said gesturing to the pair as they each raised their hand in greeting.
"Guys I have decided to call myself Bill from now on." Will told them. They turned toward him, both Chet and Carl punched him on the arm.
"Ow! What the hell was that for?" He said rubbing his aching arm.
"We are about to go after these bloody chiggers, and you want to change your name! Until this thing is over you are still gonna be known as WILL! Ok?"
"Okay Chet!"
"Sergeant Chet! If you don't mind!" Chet regretted his comment as soon as it left his mouth but the situation and the fact that he was responsible for carrying it out lay heavily on him. Carl put his finger to his lips as he looked at Will. As buddies Will would have answered him back but Chet's rank stopped him. Trey just accepted it because he was new to them and had a feeling, they all had a bit of a history together. The last man to join them was Zeb Barstow's boy Henry who had decided to go to keep an eye on his father's steers. Some of the other farmers had offered a few of their herd in addition to the Barstow brand.

Henry supplied the mounts for each of them. They were all saddled up tethered to each other in a long line. Will carried the radio while Carl checked their weapons and ammunition. He decided that none of those monsters would survive to kill any more men or animals.

"Mount up!" Chet raised his hand and signalled to move out and they headed to the stockyard on the edge of town where the cattle awaited them.

17

The ride to Red Butte was quiet. No one broke the silence. Chet led the way driving the steers with a swinging motion of his lariat and Henry brought up the rear while the others covered their flank. Henry would move back and forth sometimes breaking off to go and fetch the stragglers and bring them back to the herd and Trey broke away to retrieve the odd steer that would decide to stand belligerently nibbling on the grass until it could be coaxed into motion again.

It would take them the better part of a day to reach the Butte, so Chet decided to bed them down. It was getting dark, and they needed to make a camp. He also needed to set a watch placing each on a rota of two hours each. Carl called in every hour during the day and listening for any change in the Chigger movements. So far there was no change, all was going to plan. Chet took first watch because he felt duty bound to do it, also he was too nervous to sleep.

Henry rode around the herd cradling his rifle in the crook of his arm. His eyes scanned the gently lowing cattle watching for any sign of change. His eyes grew accustomed to the darkness, and he could discern Chet over on the other side of the herd his head was bobbing up and down as he rode. Then suddenly his head would lift and slowly droop as before.

Henry made his way carefully around the herd not making any sudden movements that would cause them to stampede and trample them to death or have to spend a lot of time rounding them up again. He reached Chet who by now was curled over his horse's neck and he reached down to take hold of Chet's reins. The sudden attention caused Chet to sit bolt upright in the saddle. Realising he had been derelict in keeping watch he muttered an apology.

Henry nodded and suggested he change over with someone who was feeling fresher. Reluctantly he headed to the camp and changed with Will. Chet unrolled his blanket and laid down. His head touched the blanket and he promptly fell asleep. When he finally awoke there was a delicious aroma of coffee in the air, and it was daylight.

Henry was pouring himself a cup and turned to Chet, he offered him the second cup he had poured. "How long have I slept Henry?" He took the cup and held his hands around the hot welcoming brew.

"Not long really we each took turns and let you sleep. It's not easy having a lot of pressure and responsibility put on you with this plan!"

"How did you know?"

"Could see how you were acting around your buddies and heard Will talking, well grousing about how you pulled rank on him in camp yesterday!"

"Yea! I did, didn't I? We had been through so much together and I went and ran off my mouth at him!"

"Don't worry about him he understood, and it was soon forgotten. He was the one who suggested we let you sleep, and he took three watches for you. Now that is the mark of a true friend!" he said as he rummaged through a bag in search for something to eat. "Incidentally, there were no sightings of the bugs, and we didn't lose any cattle during the night. I call that a result. Wouldn't you?" He said as he handed him some beef jerky.

They broke camp and doused the fire. Once more they mounted and roused the steers. The lowing cattle moved off at a steady pace. It was estimated that they would reach Red Butte in about three more hours at their present pace. Then they would have to make the corral secure and wait for the Chiggers to arrive.

Chet prayed that they were in time and that the monsters would not be planning a trap of their own.

18

Capt. Spencer sent men by chopper to the Butte to arrange the building of the corral while the cattle were being driven to their trap. By the time the herd arrived it would be open and ready. Sentries had already been posted at various vantage points overlooking the corral. The objective now was to wait for the cattle drive and the monster insects to take the bait.

***

Chet and his team felt relieved that so far, the plan had stayed on course and the cattle had been safely deposited into the corral where they happily munched on the food that had been provided. The wooden gates were shut behind them and everyone took up their positions. Orders were made for a 'cold' camp to be set up for the night which meant no fires, lights or anything that might spook the insects and everyone settled down for the evening wait. Henry gave Chet and the others some jerky to stop their stomachs from grumbling.

"Thanks Henry, sure feel empty after that ride today. I hope those bastards appreciate our food delivery service?" Chet laughed.
"I hope that they come real soon to collect. I am itching to let them see how much hot lead I am giving them for free" He gritted his teeth as he spoke.
The night passed uneventfully. Everyone involved felt disappointed at the present negative result.

Gradually, the cool morning light faded to be replaced with a hot afternoon sun.
Sweat beaded and dripped into their eyes. Their breathing became laboured as the heat shimmered. Henry's gaze never left the horizon his hat tipped low shielding the sweltering sun. Something moved, Henry peered hard at the cliff opposite. Then he heard a rasping, clicking sound and a monstrous bug raised its armoured head just above the cliff edge, silhouetted against blue sky.
Three more heads appeared. The guards saw and heard their clicking communications.

Silence fell over the camp, no one moved, no one made a sound. Any items that might create unexpected noises were held tightly secured.
Chet edged nearer to the cover of a large rock overlooking the three on the Butte. They appeared to be in no hurry. He willed them to move.
"Damn it why don't you bastards move?" He whispered.

He got his answer in the form of the cattle stampeding around the corral trying to get away from the gate where a chigger was raising itself onto the top rail.
"Fire at will!" Chet shouted, "burn them out!"
Will triggered his flamethrower and doused the gate crasher in pure flame while the others sent a hail of bullets into the lookout insects. A thick mucus and nauseating stench arose from the dying bugs. As they lay writhing Henry emptied his rifle into the sickening mess.

They had been very lucky that none of the steers had been touched but that was no consolation to Chet because intel had suggested that there were at least a possible seven sighted. The tally for today was only four.

The radio crackled into life. Capt. Spencer was asking about the skirmish.

"Four Bugs taken out sir, OVER!" Chet confirmed.
"These were smart enough to set lookouts while one tried to sneak in to grab our beef. OVER!" He continued.
"Do you think that the others might return for another try Sergeant, OVER?"
"Hmm, I would like to say no sir, but I think they may try and outflank us to get what they want. OVER!"
"Ok, your plan was a success even though you only got a few, so I am recommending a further day of waiting. Let's just see if your instinct is right? OVER!"
"Thank you, sir, OUT!" Chet felt slightly better now. At least Capt. Spencer believed he could get this done.

Chet gathered his little group around him.
"Well, it seems we have another day to get the last of the bugs. They almost got the herd. Anyone got any ideas; I am fresh out of em!"
They slowly shook their heads. Henry lifted his hat, scratched his scalp and then replaced it on his head.
"What if...?" He paused.
"What were you about to say Henry?" Chet looked up.
"Well, what if we went hunting for them instead of waiting? They won't come back here now. Those three

on the cliff seemed to be *talking* to the others. It looked too damn smart, probably a warning to stay away?"

"I would agree because they sacrificed one of their kind. Kinda felt like they were testing our numbers!"

"Where should we look? Seems to me they would have to hole up somewhere big and cool in the day and then come out when it was cooler to eat. They must have found a way to get to the top of the Butte there must be a trail of some kind up there" Chet stroked his chin.

"OK, tomorrow we split up and take a reconnoitre around the Butte. Maybe extend it a little but don't engage with them if you see them, hightail it back here. Now, get some sleep and be ready at first light."

19

Dawn broke at six that morning and the Butte shone blood red so that it lived up to its name. Chet hoisted the saddle onto the roan fastening the straps under his belly and mounted smoothly onto his broad back. They rode to the corral gates and checked on the herd. All appeared quiet. Posted sentries watched the group depart. Each one taking a different direction.
Henry took the North, Chet to the East, Carl rode South and Will to the West. Trey opted to look after the herd.

    Henry rode to the cliffside where the Chiggers had perched watching the herd milling around the corral. He spotted a flat spot that gave rise to an incline which gradually elevated onto the plateau and the cliff edge. He traced their tracks from bottom to top. Small scrub bushes and stones had been moved and crushed under their ponderous bodies.

He dismounted and peered over the edge as the lookouts had done and he was astonished to see nearly all of the encampment including the corralled animals. "Ok you bastards where are the rest of you now?"

Henry remounted after searching the immediate area around the top finding no further tracks, so it appeared that only three had come up. Taking out some binoculars from his pack he scanned the land to the right and left of his view.

A tiny figure in the distance caught his eye. It was Carl, hunched over his horse looking at the ground both right and left, he watched as the figure dismounted and knelt in the dust and appeared to study it for a while before he remounted and moved slowly forward.

***

Carl took out the Winchester from its saddle case, cocked it and held it in the crook of his arm. He had heard a scuffling in the dense bushes ahead of him and made himself ready for any confrontation. The scuffling, scraping sound got louder.

A bug reared up from the ground almost knocking him from the horse. The bay started snorting, rearing and striking out with its hooves. Carl knew he would not stand a chance of getting a clear shot at the beast because of this. In desperation he pulled hard on the reins, turning the bay he dug in his heels and took off back to the corral. The bay horse sensed his rider's commands and responded with a burst of speed worthy of a thoroughbred racehorse.

Henry had watched the events unfolding and also saw that the bug was not following Carl. It merely laid down out of sight again.

Henry rode back to camp to talk to Carl. Upon arrival at camp Henry found a radio operator and put a call into the Sheriff's office.

"Sheriff Deeds here! OVER"
"Sheriff, Henry Barstow here, I am over at Red Butte, and I need to have a word with the bug man. OVER!"
"Who? Oh yea, Dr Creed! Why do you want him? OVER"
"One of your soldier boys had a run in with one but it never followed him, just laid down all quiet like! Kinda wondered why it did that. OVER!"
"Let me get a hold of him and I will ask for you. OVER"

"As soon as you can, Sheriff as soon as you can. OUT" Henry hoped that it would not be too long before he got the answer.

20

Chet rode for some time before he saw some insect tracks. They were heading toward a stand of trees surrounded by rocks and huge boulders that formed a small cave. He dismounted, tied the reins to a bush nearby and approached on foot. He anticipated that the bug was resting in the cooling shade of the cave waiting for the sun to give way to the cooler evening air.

Upon entering he found it near the entrance looking half its normal size, still quite large but lethargic. He took careful aim and blasted half a dozen shells into its head. It reeled with each shot and its internal maw splattered all over the sandstone walls. He felt extremely satisfied, albeit slightly guilty as he had told the others to return immediately and not to engage them. Chet mounted up and rode back to camp.

Henry ran to meet him and give him his news, only for the pair to be interrupted mid conversation as the radio screeched into life.

"Sheriff Deeds to Barstow come in Barstow. Seems you were right to be suspicious Henry, those Chiggers can drop eggs when they need to. We could have a long fight on our hands! However, it is more likely to drop em when they have had a good feed. How did it look to you? OVER!"

"The one Carl saw was smaller than usual and a bit slower too, Chet just killed one in a cave a short while back and he said it was sluggish too. OVER!"

"Good! Means they aint been fed for a while and you need to kill them when they are like this. OUT"

Carl loaded up with a flamethrower while the others gathered what weapons they could and rode out to where Carl had his conflict with the chigger. It appeared to be still there, but it was getting progressively weaker, so they surrounded the bug and blasted it. Pieces of the oversized insect flew off and hit them. Carl triggered the flamethrower and reduced the splattered corpse to ash. The men gagged at the stench it created and wiped the stinking flesh from their faces as they relaxed slightly. They had taken down two of the three main chiggers down but somewhere out there one more bug was lying in wait.

21

Riding back to the camp someone asked, "Anyone seen Will?"

"No, I haven't!" was everyone's reply. Chet had been so preoccupied with the two beasts that they had killed that he never noticed Will was missing. Chet ordered them to get some shuteye. He planned to go out alone to search for Will.

Henry was determined to go with him, Carl also said he was going and would not take no for an answer, saying they had been buddies since 3rd grade and beyond and no fucking giant blood sucker was about to split them up. Secretly, Chet was pleased that he had such good friends around him. If they found Will he would be the first to call him 'Bill,' just like he wanted.

They headed West along the trail; Henry was tracking the little Pinto that Will had been allocated.

Up to now the tracks suggested that the prints were deep and heavy showing that the rider was still on its back. Small spurts of dust showing it had set of at a gallop at one point. Then they arrived at a stream where they had to go up and downstream to pick up the tracks again. Just in front and to the side of the Pinto were the tracks of the chigger with some evidence of flattened scrub and scattered stones as if it had lumbered its way along.

"Where the heck is this bastard heading? Seems to be moving away from our camp and heading back somewhere." Chet asked.

"There are no ranches down this way. Well, none I know of?" Henry replied.

They rode on silently, each one casting glances to the right and left searching for any sign that Will was near.

Chet rode on a short distance and noticed a dry creek about a hundred yards away. The edge of the bank had been crushed and pushed into the dry riverbed. Drag marks were scored deeply here. And as he rounded a slight bend he discovered the remains of the little Pinto. Of Will, there was no sign.

Chet leapt off his horse and bent to examine the corpse, he looked around warily but there was no sign of the giant either.

The others had spotted Chet getting down from the horse and did likewise. They were holding their breath in case they found their friend or the bug lying in wait for them.

Primed and ready with their weapons at the ready they approached carefully.
Chet called out that it was safe to come ahead. They breathed a sigh of relief when they did not find Will in the creek near the Pinto. However, tracks were indicating that Will had been surprised by the insect but managed to get away from it, maybe as it was feeding on his unlucky horse.

Mounting up once more they followed Will's tracks to a small pile of rocks that created a small tunnel into the hillside. As they approached the hooves scraped the rocks and a shot rang out. Chet shouted to Will that it was a search party out looking for him. Will slowly dragged himself to the cave entrance and shielded his eyes against the harsh light. "I sure am glad to see you guys" he murmured and collapsed on his face in the dust. His shirt had been torn, his face scratched and bloody and his right arm was a sodden mess where the Chigger had sprayed his arm with its chemical drool. They picked him up and gave him a drink of water and poured the rest over his arm before they bandaged him up.

He sat back groggily.

"What happened back at the dry creek?" Chet asked.

"I was checking the tracks and had my head down; the horse reared and flung me off. I think he smelled the fucker close by. Anyhow, I was about to climb back on when that sonofabitch grabbed hold of the pinto and bit its neck, next thing I knew was my arm was on fire from that shit it sprays out" Will shook his head trying to get rid of the terrifying images.

"Where is the bug now?" Chet asked.

"Last I saw it was heading back to town, it's smart Chet. It knows we tried to corner it and the bastard let the others take the fall."

"Well for now, we need to get back to camp and get you sorted out. I have to make my report to the Captain and try and explain how a bug managed to outsmart us all, something I aint relishing guys, Nosirree"

22

Will had noticed the chigger had headed toward town but had not seen it make a detour to the right where it had spotted a large buck nearby. It stopped and waited as the buck, completely unaware of its danger, calmly carried on grazing. When it had reached within six feet of the insect a solid jet of enzyme spray hit it on the heavily antlered skull and dripped into its eyes. The burning sensation made it rear up in agony and it stood stock still in confusion. The pain was so great that it was unable to move either left or right. Then a heavy weight dropped upon it. Then just effortlessly dragged its kill up to the mine where it could feast in the shade at its leisure.

***

The old miner dragged his heavily laden burro along, with an equally old rope.
'Come on Nelly quit stalling on me!'

The burro was holding back and not too keen on moving over some rocks. Nelly brayed loudly in reply to the pulling of the rope. What old Ned Dawkins did not know was that Nelly knew they were heading into danger.

Ned was a retired engineer and as a hobby loved to go into the mountains and investigate the old and long abandoned silver mines with such names as – The Lucky Strike, Tweeds Cave, or the Silver Dollar.

The latter was his destination today. Sometimes he was lucky enough to find a discarded nugget or two, other days he would walk through the mines and not find a dimes worth or there would be a cave in and therefore it was not worth his time trying to dig his way through for some spare change.

As Ned approached the entrance to the Silver Dollar he noticed that the entrance had a fresh mark on the timber prop to the right of the doorway. He had never noticed it last time he was here and thought someone else was prospecting like himself.
He tied a struggling Nelly to an old post, switched on his lamp and ventured inside.
He saw that the dirt on the floor had been disturbed but there were no firm boot prints only scuff marks. As he turned to the right the light picked up a large shiny surface and he heard a sucking noise.

Ned was horrified to see a deer slowly being drained of its life-giving blood. The huge insect stopped for a moment, held in check by the light of Ned's lamp. He dropped it, turned and fled out of the mine, untied and mounted his pony and hightailed it away from the gruesome sight. Clattering over rocks they went kicking up dust and stones. Nelly stumbled over a rock, her hoof knocking a piece from it. Looking back, saw they were clear and dismounted to check on his burro. Nelly stood patiently while Ned checked out each one of her hooves. He heard a scuffling and looked up to see the giant insect head coming out of the mine.

"We best get out of here Nelly before that thing gets us!" He said as he jumped onto a rock and swing himself into the saddle before he grabbed Nelly's tether and took off rapidly. He hoped to put enough space between himself and the bug. The slope was getting steeper, and Ned was standing in his stirrups urging his horse on the most hair-raising trip it had ever encountered.

At last, the ground levelled out and he had a clear path from out of the tree line.
He spotted a group of people in the distance and raced toward them, whooping and hollering to get their attention. They reined in and watched as the distant rider approached.

"Stop! Stop! You fellers are heading into trouble!" He shouted.

"What is he saying?" Will asked.

"Sounds like he is saying stop go back something about trouble?"

Ned brought Nelly to a stop just in front of the group. "Boys there is a giant bug up there holed up in the old Silver Dollar mine! That sonofabitch is huge, and I was lucky it was feeding on a buck. Darn near got me and Nelly here!"

"Did you just say you saw a chigger in a mine?" Chet exclaimed in surprise.

"Damn, how the fuck did it get around us Chet?" Carl said as he scanned the distance.

"I told you it was smart didn't I?" Will beamed.

"Ok so where do you think it would go next?" Carl asked.

"I reckon it would take a nap after its meal and then go look for more?" Will rubbed his chin thoughtfully.

"First things first we get you to a medic to get that arm of yours fixed!" Said Chet firmly.

23

Back in town at the sheriff's office Wilbur sat in his favourite chair, a glass of Jack Daniels in. He just stared at it, turning it to and fro watching the light twinkling through the amber liquid as he thought to himself how in the hell did they end up in this situation.
His radio crackled into life.
"Sheriff Deeds! Wilbur are you there? Pick up please. Over!"
"Deeds here over!"
"Elmer here. Wilbur, I have been doing some research and if my findings are correct I've got some bad news for you. The remaining insect is a female! I repeat that the last chigger is female and is going to lay her eggs soon. We are talking about thousands of little bastards! Over!"
"Damn Elmer, we need to find her before she lays those eggs, chances are she's holed up in a mine.

Some old prospector ran into a search party of National Guard talking about a giant bug up in a mine and they radioed it in. Over"

"Wilbur, you need to pass the information on to them. It will be crucial that they finish the female off before there are more of them and we get overrun. Over."

Wilbur placed his drink down on the desk untouched. He took his hat from the rack and made his way out through the office doors.

24

As Chet and the search party reached the camp they heard a lot of noise. Both gunfire and shouting filled the air. The corralled steers were lowing in extreme panic and trying to stampede hurling themselves against the timber fence that held them in. At this point, they couldn't see what was causing all the fuss. Then a few fist sized lumps moved away from one of the soldiers.
"Damn it, this chigger has young uns! I thought it wuz supposed to lay eggs?" Chet swore.
"Looks like they sorta skipped out a couple of stages."
    Chet contacted headquarters informing them that for now they had driven the offspring back in the direction of the mine. They had used fire and grenades to good effect. The stench of charred black ticks was overpowering. It made their eyes water, and the rank smoke left an acrid taste in their dry mouths.

Up at the Silver Dollar, the primary female was resting. Some of her young were exploring the tunnels when they saw daylight and headed out into the light. These hard ticks were moving like an oily black wave marching steadily down from Eagle Mountain into the sparse sage brush on the hunt for fresh blood to feed on. As they reached an area of long grass they disappeared. Each one had selected stalks as a vantage point. Now all they had to do was wait, for any unsuspecting animal to walk by and brush up against the predators and provide them with a tasty meal.

A mountain lion out with her cubs spotted a wild turkey. She went into stealth mode. As she approached the bird it sensed the danger and burst through the brush a mountain lion in hot pursuit. The male cub decided to investigate a movement on a nearby branch only to find that he had acquired a tick. Its bite on his neck made him stumble and cry out with intense pain and fear.

The lioness stopped in her tracks and turned at her cub's distress call. The bird stopped running as soon as it thought its danger had passed, only to have a few ticks latch onto it, the defenceless creature's life was over quickly. Not so the little cubs.

She attempted to swipe a couple of ticks away but more appeared to take their place before one managed to get a hold on her leg. She stopped for a moment to try and bite it off, but the enzyme was working quickly now, and more ticks came in their oily wave to cover her. At last, she faded and lost her valiant attempt to save her cub.

However, the other cub, a female, watched and heard the wailing of the vain battle. She backed away keeping low just like her mother taught her when danger was close by. She slowly retreated until she felt a hard rock ledge touch her back and stopped discovering an abandoned rabbit hole, where she hid. The ticks dropped to the ground sated from their meal of mountain lion.

25

Wilbur jumped into the driving seat of the commandeered vehicle and roared off to Sheraton Chemicals. He was eager to see if the scientist had managed to achieve the solution to the nightmare that was being presented to them. The idea that the female was producing offspring was making him break out into sweats. His hands started shaking as he grabbed the wheel. His knuckles were so tight they appeared white and cracked audibly as he took the twists and turns of the country roads. He felt as though he had run a marathon the last few days, his head throbbed, and he could feel exhaustion starting to set in. Wilbur pulled up in a cloud of dust and leapt out, shutting the door behind him with a slam. He burst through the glass door in front of him and without waiting, made his way straight to Dr. Creed's laboratory.

"I know the way!' He shouted over his shoulder, effectively causing the receptionist's jaw to drop before she could say anything. He found Elmer's door and called his name before entering. The door slowly shut behind him.

"Wilbur! Glad you came! I may have some good news for you?' He offered a hand as he spoke. We managed to get a couple of the young ones sent over, live ones and they are proper nasty little buggers. They would take your hand off if they got the chance.. once they get a sniff of meat they go into a feeding frenzy. I want you to watch this.." He said as he led Wilbur over to a clear plastic box with a small slit in the top.

Wilbur saw a black fist sized blob in the corner. It looked harmless just sitting there. Elmer took a piece of raw, bloody meat from another plastic box, as he opened the lid the black blob became agitated scrabbling and clawing frantically, trying to get at the raw meat which was about a foot away from the trapped tick. As the tick became agitated Wilbur was so shocked at the burst of speed that he almost fell over backwards in retreat "Shiiiiit! Elmer that was scary?"

"Yep sure was. Bugger caught me out the first time I did it. Now watch this!" He used a small spray bottle and squirted a clear liquid into the box and after a minute it dropped, and its legs began trembling. Finally, they stopped, and the body split open spilling its innards over the bottom of the box.

Wilbur was speechless for a moment, "Wow! That's what we need." He said at last.

"Well, don't get your hopes up just yet this formula works on these things but may not work on the female. We won't know for sure until we test it though."

Wilbur nodded in reply, "Last I heard she was holed up inside the Silver Dollar mine?"

"If I can pressurise this or make it viable as a gas then we could seal up the mine and fill it with this formula" Elmer rubbed his palms together in anticipation of a good result.

"I won't ask you what you are using in that spray Doc. Just get it ready as soon as you can and let me know. We can get it airlifted up to the mine. I can get the army guys to seal up the exits in readiness!" Wilbur shook his hand and then took his leave. The ride back to Calico was a bit more relaxed, Wilbur's grip on the wheel was a bit less tense in comparison to his arrival. He distinctly felt a surge of hope.

26

Chet received his orders to get his fire team into position to support the engineers. Their objective was to keep the insects holed up inside the mine while charges were placed within the entrances. Several fireteams were needed to cover all the necessary exits. Each time the black tide tried to leave, a fierce jet of fire and hot lead was sprayed until they backed away into the dark recesses of the mine. During the lull engineers ran inside and set up their equipment frantically looking around checking for the return of the voracious insects. Five exits were found, and the deadly charges were set. At a synchronised signal they were all triggered, the resulting explosion rocked the land for miles around, the exits collapsed, finally sealing the bugs inside. Then, as one, all of the fireteams pumped the air cheering.

Dr Creed had supplied the chemical that was to be dispersed in an attempt to disable and hopefully kill off the gigantic infestation.

As the air inside the mine gradually filled with gas the black ticks started to drop, their legs twitching and antennae rapidly slowing down to finally succumb to the pesticide. Some managed to scuttle back through the tunnels to the main chamber where the large female was patiently waiting. She felt the effects of the gas on her giant body and legs, she rubbed them together trying to rub the burning sensation away as she watched the smaller insects falling victim to the gas. She turned and scuttled back into the darkness.

Her survival instincts had served her well as she noticed a glimmer of light to the left of her position and headed toward it. The air felt warmer as she neared the hole and bracing herself pushed hard until the rocky edge finally gave under the strain and burst forth in a cloud of dust and broken rock.
She struggled to push her large and bloated body through the gap. The pesticide was slowly eating its way through the carapace causing multiple burns where it had landed.

27

The still cheering fireteams had no idea that the largest female had managed to escape the trap. Orders were relayed to stand down that their objective had been achieved. Chet turned to his team, "I have a bad feeling about this?"
"Why Sarge? The op was a success, wasn't it?" Will asked.
"I just have a cold feeling is all and I think I need to see the body!"
"How? That sucker will be buried under a ton of rock by now?" Carl asked.
"Too easy boys! It doesn't feel right to me!" Chet told them before they headed back to the camp at the butte.

***

The female laid quietly on the dusty ground. Instinctively she scooped the loose material over her burning body. Feeling almost instant relief as the dry earth landed on her. She was hungry and her antenna moved to and fro, searching for any sound or vibration which would signal a fresh source of sustenance. She wanted to produce more offspring to replace those taken from her within the mine. She suddenly stopped and focussed on a sound of animals in a particular area, the cattle were lowing very loudly protesting at their being confined in a small corral. She dragged herself toward the sound.

***

The laboratory at Sheraton Chemicals was a hive of activity. White coated Technicians with protective eye-shields and clipboards scurried around like bees carrying pollen back to the hive. Sometimes two would meet head on and have to do a twostep to avoid encroaching on each other's progress. Each technician would approach just one man the major domo that was Dr. Creed. He could be seen directing the operations much like a cop controlling traffic. He would send each technician scurrying back and forth to adjust the huge mixing machines producing the batches of chemicals that made up the much sought after solution to the bug problem. So far the feedback suggested that this batch was more successful than the last one he prepared. However, he felt that this present batch needed further testing but there were no more subjects to test it on and in frustration found himself barking at the technicians before he finally headed out of the lab. He walked swiftly to his office, head bowed not wishing to make eye contact or conversation along the way. He had just put his hand on the office door when Gina his receptionist happened to look up from her typing.

"You okay Elmer?"

"Jeez, Gina I was a bit lost in my thoughts there! Damn near jumped clean out of my body?" He said as made an attempt at a laugh.

"Come on, I have known you a long time, I can tell when you got something heavy on your mind. Is it those bug things?" She asked as she got up from her desk and approached him and placed her well, manicured fingers gently on his arm. He could smell her perfume. She wore lily of the valley, and he noticed that since buying her some for her birthday she would never wear any other brand. Gina was a good-looking lady for her age, unmarried and the wrong side of forty she would say if anyone dared to ask her age. She had a soft spot for Elmer and often wondered if he had felt as strongly about her as she felt for him. Elmer felt the warmth of her hand and gave it a gentle pat then planted a light kiss on her cheek. Gina blushed like she was sixteen again. Her hand touched her cheek and paused there.

"Why Elmer, I do declare, I hope your intentions are purely honourable." She laughed. Elmer loved to hear her laugh. It was refreshing to his ears.

"Coffee Elmer?" She giggled.

"Sure thing Gina and make it strong!" He entered the office a bit more positively. He sat looking at the days figures and pulled the phone nearer. He picked up the phone and called the sheriff's office.

"Wilbur, it's Elmer, look I need to get out into the field again. I want to catch a couple more of the bugs, this latest batch is untested and according to my calculations the previous batch may not be very effective and just wear off after a while. Can you arrange with the guard for us to go on a reconnoitre of the situation. I mean would they sanction it?

"Well, I am sure if we stress that it is to monitor the chemical results of our last test it shouldn't be a problem. Let me get back to you on that okay"

Wilbur put in his call to the General and explained their latest plan. The general was reluctant at first to agree as he thought it might put them in a dangerous position if the situation was at that point unknown. Wilbur used his verbal skills the kind that could only be honed after the many years of courtroom experience he had gained and had never lost an argument, well hardly ever. He arranged for a Huey chopper to go to Sheraton Chemicals where he and Dr. Creed were to be picked up and flown to the last known area of infestation, the mine.

    Wilbur phoned Elmer with the good news. He left the office and headed to Sheraton Chemical plant for the rendezvous with the chopper. He pulled up in the carpark to find the helicopter waiting for him, its rotors softly spinning, engine and tail idling. Elmer was already inside and seated opposite two hard jawed, stony faced GI's with AK 47s draped across their knees. Wilbur took in the KA-BAR knives in leg sheaths strapped to their legs as he climbed in the cabin and took his seat. The engine revolutions screamed as the helicopter launched into the air.

    Wilbur's ears popped with the change in pressure and the pilot turned his head to speak. He pointed to the headset hanging near his head and the pilot mimed for it him to put it on. Elmer noticed and did the same.

"Okay Sheriff where do you wish to go?" The voice crackled in his ears.

"Take us to the last known coordinates of the chigger sightings." The pilot turned into the wind and headed west toward the Silver Dollar mine.

The pilot put the Huey down on a space no bigger than half a football field. It touched down gently. Wilbur and Elmer had tried to engage their escorts in conversation, but they were both tight lipped. Wilbur turned to Elmer and gave him some observations.

"Ya know Elmer our two good ole boys here I believe are Navy Seals! They don't have any insignia on their uniforms, see. They got those earpieces and throat mikes so we can't hear them. Of course, my friend Colonel Waite keeps me well informed, he mentioned that we would have couple of babysitters. Old Iron Balls said it was in case we hijacked their transport!" he chuckled. Elmer started laughing.

As they stepped out, one of the soldiers said "Sheriff you are one wily ole fox and yeah we are SEALS, no names though as we like it that way! We will take the lead and check it out before we bring you up. You ok with that? If not, tough cookies that's how it is we ain't playing!"

"Oh, don't worry son we wouldn't dream of crossing the cream of the crop!" Wilbur shot a quick wink to Elmer.

One of the escorts got off with them, his weapon held across his chest. He scanned the area checking to make sure the coast was clear and the three of them moved out and made their way over to the camp. Elmer interviewed some of the engineers who had set the charges. It was painstaking having to gather intelligence this way, but the escorts hurried them along.

"Not much to go on here Wilbur, the mine is sealed but I would like to be sure it is over at last." As if on cue they noticed the SEAL escort running back to them.

"Got some intel on a large object heading for the corral at Red Butte" He told the pair.

"Yea! We laid a trap for them over there a couple of days ago but one got away. I think it managed to get outta the mine. Question is did it take any young uns with her?" Wilbur replied, hoping that wasn't the case.

"Wilbur! If she managed to feed there is a good chance she will lay more damn eggs and we have to go through this nightmare all over again!" Elmer spoke, concern clearly evident in his voice.

"Ok, gentlemen back to the chopper and we will head over to Red Butte!" one of the seal replied.

Elmer and Wilbur became out of breath very quickly as they had tried to run while the SEAL just loped along like he was out for a stroll. The escort who had remained on board extended a hand and pulled the tired pair in, as Wilbur fell inside, the Huey took off.

28

The scene at Red Butte corral was brutal, the teams were caught unawares, the steers were circling inside their enclosure trying their best to avoid being a victim to the bug, but the bellowing and stamping did not help them. The insect just lifted and dropped on three steers covering them in its toxic fluids. The feeding frenzy began in earnest. Fire teams tried to shoot her, but the exoskeleton was proving much stronger than previous encounters, and nothing happened when a sustained burst of flammable liquid hit her at point blank range. The soldier who had been close to the insect was grabbed by the insect and chopped in two.

She threw the pieces contemptuously onto her present meal and devoured it as if he were merely a dessert. The teams were shocked at the ferocity of the beast. A concentrated burst of white-hot rage erupted on behalf of their dead comrade and animated them into a flurry of bullets and flame discharged in her direction. It just had no effect on her at all.

The chopper arrived just as the fight broke out and hovered above a clearing, giving the men inside a clear view of the carnage unfolding below.
"Good God! She appears to be indestructible now, her exoskeleton must have evolved to the point where bullets and flame are not effective anymore!" Elmer gasped. The SEALS were logging everything and fired their weapons in the chiggers direction, striking it multiple times upon its body, to no avail. Confirming Elmer's fears. They signalled to each other to move out and to escort their charges away from the danger. They took off. On the ground Chet gave the order to retreat to a safe distance and regroup to wait for fresh orders. He felt sickened to his stomach that the plan had failed. By the time the intel reached the superiors the female had taken her fill and settled down to rest. Her next task was to provide eggs and a fresh set of offspring for her brood. In the chopper, Elmer and Wilbur asked to be returned to the laboratory and the escorts found themselves briefing their commanders

on the situation. Elmer had explained to them that he needed to get some eggs or hatchlings to test the upgraded chemical solution. Unless this happens and soon it may be too late. Fortunately, Elmer's words of warning were heeded and a plan to send in a group of elite troops to carry out the dangerous assignment was set into motion.

    A six-man team, call sign Alpha 6, checked over their equipment before they climbed aboard the Huey, all six were seasoned men. They had seen more action than any soldier, to them this assignment was just another day at the beach. As before no badges, no identification of any kind on show only their dog tags were to be allowed for this one. Code names Alpha 1&3 were to be first in for the egg snatch while 2&4 next, then finally 5&6 to cover them should the insect realise what was going on and decide to retaliate. If 1&3 were successful the eggs were to be placed in a plastic cage that Elmer had supplied for them and then cover would be provided for 2&4. Flash bangs were to be employed for distraction and sleeping gas canisters for any heavy activity of the deadly female. Although it was hoped that their stealth techniques worked heavily in their favour.

    She had laid quietly after her surfeit of steers and slept soundly. Alpha 1&2 left their weapons with the group having decided that the sling rings would create enough noise to wake the sleeping giant. And as they often said, 'discretion is the better part of valour.' Alpha 1 managed to work his way round to her rear and made a tentative look underneath. Damn it! There is nothing there yet! He thought to himself.

He turned using the signal to abort, drawing a finger across his throat. Alpha 3 replied using two fingers pointed at his own eyes then back to him, then again. Alpha 1 turned to see mama's hind leg twitch and flick, so near it almost hit him. Moments later three gelatinous globes dropped in the dust of the corral. Alpha 1 opened the box and dropped one slippery blob into it. He tried to close the lid quickly but discovered that the container was slightly undersized and pushed down hard, it squashed the egg flat against the square sides. There was an audible click as the catch fastened, they paused for a moment studying the insect, hoping the noise had not disturbed it from its slumber. Nothing. Alpha1 almost let out a huge sigh of relief but remembering where he was, ran toward number 3 who passed him on the way as he went to retrieve another egg.

Two down and some more to go.

"Alpha 2&4 you're up next. Eggs are bigger now so you need to push down on that box lid good an hard" Alpha 1 informed the pair.

"Roger that!" Alpha 2 replied. Approaching very quietly and carefully they too managed to secure their objectives. While there they observed a mass of translucent material piled up and getting higher each minute. By the time they passed the last team, the pile had spilled over, and more eggs were being deposited on top. Alpha 5 slipped on the delivered offspring and landed on his back covered in the sticky mucus. Alpha 6 picked up an egg and managed to box it up. He then turned his attention to his fallen comrade.

Extending a gloved hand toward him, he paused as he spotted movement made by the female. Eggs dropped onto Alpha 5 trapping him. Fortunately, being coated in her birthing material, his own scent was masked. she adjusted her body to allow more eggs to drop to the ground. In that brief movement Alpha 5 grabbed Alpha 6 and pulled with every ounce of strength he had and finally released himself from the sticky sucking mess. He almost dropped a hastily grabbed egg and placed it into his box. Alpha 6 stood on it clipping it into place. They raced away from the scene both deciding that there was no looking or turning back. Alpha team had made it back safely with their precious cargo and the Huey took off, turning as it climbed and headed for the Sheraton laboratory.

Alpha 5 sat quietly his box held firmly on his lap. Sometimes mucus dripped from his vest and made a plopping sound as it landed on the floor. As a SEAL he had an air of stoicism. No expression, no wrinkling of the nostrils or wiping the excess material from his person. There was no ribaldry from the others just a stony stare that suited the present occasion.

The chopper touched the ground gently. They jumped out and marched stolidly to the awaiting team. Silently they handed them over.
Alpha 1 broke the silence for the first time, "Doctor Creed, these eggs were much bigger than you had encountered, so we jammed them in. I hope this has not affected the contents too much?" They turned about and were about to leave when Elmer noticed Alpha 5 and the mucus.
"Could I have a sample of that stuff on you fella?"
"Affirmative Doc. Take as much as you need, I have lots to spare! I think I have it right up my wazoo" Elmer laughed. The SEALS laughed too, released from the constraints of the mission.
Everyone had to endure the safety protocols that stripped them and made sure they had not picked up anything that would prove harmful to their deadly chemical cocktail. Alpha 5 was just glad to get a free

wash and blow and valeting of his uniform. The mucus having been removed carefully to study its DNA. Its present location was on a slide under a microscope in the farthest laboratory on the complex. Another sample was in a Petri dish in a growth medium while yet more were in other such dishes with various concoctions of chemicals that would make it react by killing it on a molecular level. The eggs meanwhile were being studied by Elmer emptying the boxes and the contents released into a much larger tank. No eggs were badly crushed, and the chigger juniors were not harmed, well not yet. Normal size chigger eggs would hatch within six to seven days. However, these chiggers no one knew how quickly they would hatch or feed.

Elmer knew that time was of the essence, from the intel the SEALS mentioned the female had already laid at least a few dozen eggs. Hopefully they had time before they put in an appearance!

29

Chet and his team were on a rota all through the day and night. Each one of them just itching to light up the bitch of a bug that was crouching in their corral right now. Chet dismantled and cleaned his weapon every hour. As he checked it over for about the twentieth time, Carl reached a hand over and enclosed his magazine, "You gonna wear the slide out afore ya done Sarge." Chet looked up and a grin split his face. "Hell yea, yer right. I guess I'm wound tighter than a clock spring. It's this damn waitin gettin to me!"
A comms tech approached Chet and handed him a piece of paper.
"Dang it ya chigger bastard!" He exclaimed.

Everyone's head turned in his direction. They waited for him.

"Boys, I got word that our buddy Will was flown to the hospital where he had surgery on that arm. Seems the arm couldn't be saved because the Chigger 'spit' burned him to the bone! I had Jinksy on the comms do a little follow up on the quiet line! I got a personal vendetta on this bug now?"

"We hear ya Sarge and we are all with ya on that score!" Carl replied looking around at all of the nodding heads.

***

Dr Creed looked at the eggs in their sterile plastic boxes. Backlit in order to watch the developing embryos closely. In the first hour, they appeared as dark grey dots that seemed to hang inside the bio luminescent egg sac. Hour two and the dots started moving, bouncing from side to side, appearing and disappearing as they moved from the light source. By the third, threads appeared to form limbs that flailed against the sac. Hour four, he observed a pulsating movement from within the cages. The egg sacs were shrinking, hardening. Hours five and six the sacs split, and the chiggers emerged. They all appeared sluggish and resorted to nibbling on their cast-off sac casing.

Elmer held pieces of raw meat which had been injected with the new batch of toxin over one of the Perspex boxes and observed a frenzy not unlike that of a gathering of sharks when the water was laced with chum. The hatchling grabbed at the meat and gorged on every morsel. Moments later there was a jerking and twitching which stopped as quickly as it started. An eerie silence fell as each scientist went over to the box to check. No one wanted it to revive, so they kept a very close eye on the specimen for over an hour. Elmer donned some thick rubber gloves that extended all the way to his elbows then reached in tentatively in case it should arouse itself. Holding it gingerly he brought it to the cold steel of a table and took a scalpel then proceeded to cut it open. The graunching sound as the blade made its way through the tough thorax made Elmer cringe, then prying the exoskeleton apart he made his observations. The hatchlings' internal organs were split in places. This was an unexpected result. The chemicals on their own worked in differing ways but together they caused aneurysms of the delicate membranes that carried the body fluids around the organism. Elmer tossed the carcass into a container and sealed it.

  Next step was to inject more meat and get the largest bug to eat it. However, there was a huge drawback as Elmer realised that these eggs had hatched quickly and that now, there would be many more young roaming free now.

30

The lethal cocktail was quickly dispatched to the Red Butte frontline where Chet received his orders alongside a batch of preloaded syringes. A number of steers had been butchered to provide as many portions as they could handle, and teams were set up to inject each portion.

Chet arranged his men at suitable points around the corral and portions of the drug laced meat were thrown into the fast, developing ticks. There was a cacophony of rustling and scurrying of tiny bodies eager to get at the meat and to gorge upon this unexpected feast.

The meat did not last long as the voracious youngsters sucked it down leaving any bones that may have been present in the hard packed dust. The adult female made no attempt to approach the meat and watched as the youngsters fought over the remnants. It seemed as if she was assessing the situation. Gradually a small pile of young ticks built up, legs twitching and eventually becoming still, she moved her back legs pushing against the pile until they were smashed to a pulp. The female bug lifted her bulky body on her front legs and hauled herself toward the wooden rails that formed the corral dropping onto the topmost timber. There was a loud crack as it took the full weight of the bug and it fell neatly to the ground. She gradually dragged herself out of the corral, her antennae manically searching for more food.

    Her senses were heightened as her hunger grew in intensity. She covered a lot of ground before the guards could stop her. Rearing up she spit her enzymes toward the soldiers, who tried to dodge the spurts of acidic fluid. Several were hit on the head, luckily their faces were protected by their helmets, but the drips were falling onto cloth covered shoulders and arms. Even running down over their chest where it would find its way under the bulletproof vests they wore.

Screams of intense burning pain filled the air as they tried to remove their vests and clothing before they succumbed to the melting effects of the bugs acid. The other men ran for safety, knocking and pushing each other in fear and one tripped over a rock. The bug reached him before he could get back to his feet. It grabbed him and the man screamed, as a long tendril probed at his face before it slipped into his mouth, releasing a burst of acid down his throat turning his insides to liquid. Moments later the same tendril sucked the innards soup from the body. It tore the man in half and carelessly tossed the remains aside.

***

The horned owl sat silently atop a tall cactus waiting. Its head swivelled to and fro listening to the sounds of the night. Cicadas chirruped and the odd packrat would venture out to forage. She spotted her prey and silently glided over the ground. As she extended her talons, the pack rat sensed that danger was near and took off in a quick burst of speed dodging over and around bushes and rocks with the owl keeping pace. The couple of times the talons were within grasping range a sudden twist and it took off in another direction. In the dim light it noticed a small hole and hit it at full tilt just as the owl reached it.

Realising that its meal was gone, the owl silently turned aside to return to its observation post on top of the cactus and folded its wings.

The pack rat poked its head out from the safety of the rocks and decided the coast was clear. As it exited a burst of corrosive acid sprayed from within the hole. It caught the packrat on the back. In an instant it had lost all feeling in its hind legs and a voracious young chigger was gradually demolishing the body from back to front. Only the bones that held the skin and internal organs would be recognisable as having once been a living breathing animal.

The instant meal provided the necessary energy to attempt to enlarge the hole. Small pebbles were obstructing the exit stopping her getting out of the confining space when a sudden shift in a pebble created a bit more space to manoeuvre her fast growing and thickening body. The frenzy she had felt left her and became overtaken by an irresistible urge to sleep, to conserve what energy she had.

31

As Chet toyed with the fire sending sparks into the night sky like miniature fireworks a startled voice crackled from the radio, "Able one to Able two, Able one to Able two over!" Chet grabbed the headset placed a speaker to his ear and spoke into the attached microphone.
"Able two to Able one receiving you over!"
"Able two, the female is laying more eggs. I repeat female is laying more eggs! But the plates on her back are splitting, Again I repeat the female's back is splitting. Standing by for further instructions. Over."
Chet jumped up and down whooping and hollering.

The others just stared at his reactions in complete surprise.

"Able one, hold your position. Just hold your position! We are on our way over!" Chet said quickly, throwing the headset and radio down.

"Boys! That huge fucker is splitting and producing more of those little bastards, and we are about to drop some heavy shit down on it. I said I was gonna get it and here is the ideal time to do it." He said, as he grabbed a couple of grenades and then gave the group orders to do the same. They made their way to the female's rear and saw for himself the splitting of the back plates.

Getting close to the back end of a voracious bug and risking life and limb was not something you did every day, but Chet was like a man possessed. He jumped onto her back and pulled the pin from one of the grenades then threw it into the crack that was emerging. Once completed he turned and ran, narrowly missing being caught in the blast in the process. The others used this moment to their advantage and threw their grenades at the insect in rapid succession. The subsequent explosions tore the exposed beast into huge lumps of burned flesh, the eggs she laid also being consumed in fire.

    The radio crackled into life once more and Chet reported the demise of the giant bug when a chance opening appeared. He admitted that there was no time to consult with his superiors and would take full responsibility for his actions. Another team was dispatched to confirm the kill and to clean up any and all stragglers.

Chet gathered his equipment and swung his leg casually over his hired mount. Swinging the horse's head he made his way down the trail back to Calico closely followed by the group. As they rode back no one spoke. They were too tired to care. Chet tossed a comment over his shoulder, "At least this nightmare is over now!"

On the other side of the Silver Dollar mine, a fat and extremely pregnant female bug finally squeezed herself out into the sunshine and headed off in search of food to support her future offspring. She stopped when she heard movement up ahead

LESTER

Time: 8:10 a.m. 9/27/1989

"Lester!"

"Yes Momma!"

"Look here, I have to go into Jefferson and pay yo Daddy's medical bill, I need you to be good and look after Charlie for me? Now it's a big responsibility an I don't want you getting into any trouble now ya hear?"

"Yes Momma! I will look after Charlie for you and Daddy. I promise."

"See that you do child cos if I hear you let him loose I will take you to the woodshed and you know whut happens there don't ya?"

"I sure do, I get whupped! Don't I Momma?"

Jessie Raines stifled a giggle at the reply. In all of Lester's twelve-year-old life he was only ever threatened with the woodshed. He knew he had a good Mom and she loved him and his seven-year-old brother. He would never step over the line like other boys did.

He saw them come from a woodshed with tears in their eyes, he vowed never to get that way.

Jessie got her finest going to church clothes and got ready to take the trip to the hospital to see her sick husband Terrance. He had been taken to hospital when his appendix burst, and old Doc Morris arranged for an operation – unfortunately it was going to cost a lot of money…$4000 to be precise.

Jessie worked hard and managed to scrape it together and leaving the children was heart wrenching in itself. She saw Granny Haswell on her porch and greeted her.

"Mornin Granny! How's your rheumatism today?"

"Oh same as always chile thanks fer askin!" Granny replied. Her rocking chair creaking back and forth on the old wooden floor.
Jessie stopped for a moment and lowered her head.

"What's up honey?" Granny looked kindly on Jessie like another daughter.

"Gotta go into Jefferson to pay Terry's hospital bill Granny! I have to leave Charlie and Lester alone in the house!" Jessie's voice started to crack.

"Granny! Would you keep an eye on them while I'm gone?"

"Why chile you know I will look after yo fine boys, I'll keep em out of mischief. You just go and see yo man an tell him Ole Granny wants him to shift his ass an get back home! It's bin too long!" Granny cackled and it made her cough.

"Bye Granny! See you later!" Jessie moved off, waving until she was out of sight.

In town three people were engrossed in conversation.
Max Quigley, Frank Duchesne, Opie Cleveland and the only girl in the gang – Coraline Rivers.

"Quiggy I heard that Jessie Raines has money saved up and hidden in the house!" Frankie Duchesne stammered. Frankie was scrawny to the point of skeletal. This was due to the drugs that took in vast quantities.. when he could get them. And usually it was other folks that provided the cash. He would target people and break into their homes, steal what he could to fund his nasty habit.

His teeth were crooked and rotten, and his clothes just hung in rags on him.

Max or Quiggy as he was known was a knife wielding thug who terrorised the neighbourhood getting into fights with local gangs and robbing any innocent traveller along the way.

Opie Cleveland was a wannabe. He wanted to be a gangster, a member of a feared troupe of thieves and vagabonds. Max tolerated him because his Dad was the town's Druggist and Opie could get some gear for the gang.

Coraline Rivers, a wild child as you might say and a runaway to boot. She had left home at ten years old to get away from an abusive father only to end up with an abusive boyfriend named Max. She was fourteen now.

Coraline had endured physical and mental abuse from Max and suffered a miscarriage when Max punched her in a drug induced rage. Coraline was also too scared to leave in case Max decided to kill her. Max also had psychopathic traits. A spell in a penitentiary and under the watchful eyes of a psychiatrist determined his profile.

Unfortunately, all this was before Coraline had met and fell under the spell of Max Quigley.

"How much do ya reckon she has hid?" Max looked deep into Frankie's eyes, they were blue, and the pupils were dark pin pricks.

"Dunno! But I heard people say she had four grand?" He scratched at his scruffily bearded face nervously.

"Ok! Where she live?" Max sneered.

"Canyon Road, right on the end" Frankie gushed.

"Ok, we go to Dixie's bar and get a drink first?"

"I gotta get back fore the ole man misses me Quiggy?" Opie dragged his boot in the dust.

"Go on then baby face, fuck off and let the men sort it out!" He snarled.

Opie felt like he had been doused in ice water.

"I can sneak out later, meet ya in an hour or two?"

"Ok! Want you at the start of Canyon Road at ten? Ok?"

Opie nodded his head rapidly, "Shure Max I will be there!"

Max just glared as Opie ran off.

Nine o clock and Dixie's bar filled to the brim with dirty bikers and the flotsam and jetsam of society. No smart person would ever drink in this bar. It was a dive. Fights often broke out over the slightest thing. Furniture was broken usually over the clientele. The barkeep kept a shotgun with a sawn-off end under the bar and wasn't afraid to use it when keeping order.

Max ordered bourbon for three. They sat in the corner. Max sat with his back against the wall and facing the door. It was a favoured spot because Max liked to see what trouble may be coming his way and he just might have the edge.

"Couple more drinks and we can slip out through the toilets so no one can see us go" then slip back same way – alibi sorted ok?"

"OKAY?" Max suddenly bellowed in Frankie's ear. Frankie almost shit himself at the volume his ear drum received.

"Fuck me Quiggy! That almost made me deaf!" Max rolled back his head and laughed.

After creeping out of Dixie's making sure they weren't spotted, they made their way to Canyon Road, where Opie was hidden in a bush.

"What the f.. are you doing in that bush baby face?" Max said

"Keeping out of sight Quiggy! Too many people coming along so I hid here!" Opie whined.

"Never mind, let's go!"

They walked slowly watching for anyone who might see them together, but all appeared quiet.

They stood looking up at the Jessie's house and saw a light on in the parlour. Max crept up to the window and spotted the two boys seated on an old dusty couch each with a bowl of cereal and a spoon eating and laughing.

He tried the door and the handle turned very slowly. The door was pushed open, and he walked into the room. Lester jumped up and pulled Charlie behind him.

"What y'all want?" He asked boldly swelling his chest trying to look bigger.

"Where's the money kid?" Max stepped toward Lester threateningly.

"What money? We aint got no money – I got ten cents in my pocket though!" He spoke.

"I shall ask you again – where is the fucking money?" This time Max used his knife to forcefully present the question.

"I tole you mister we aint got no money!"

"Got no money!" Echoed Charlie.
Max lunged and caught Charlie by his collar and put his knifepoint at Charlie's throat.

"Frankie! Search the house top to bottom!"

"Boy! If you don't tell me I am gonna slice this here little un! Now don't mess with me!"

Lester's eyes started to glisten, and a tear rolled down his face, "I aint/ we aint got any money in the house!" Lester insisted through huge sobs.

"What about the four grand I heard about?" Max glared.

"Oh that! Momma took that this morning to Jefferson Hospital to pay for Daddy's bill!" Lester felt relieved because no money they might just leave them be.

"Arrrghhh! Fuckin too late!" Max screamed and lashed out, his knife slashed Charlie under the chin and the blood gushed from the severed jugular.

Lester jumped at Max and managed to get his nails raking across his eyes and Max in a fury stabbed Lester. There was a stunned silence as the gang realised that Max had killed two children his knife had been grabbed by Lester in self-defence, but such was the force he had pulled it back to ram it into the boy's neck.

Stumbling around he found an oil lamp and smashed it on the floor while it was lit, and flame and oil spread throughout in a matter of moments. The gang fled as the flames engulfed the little wooden house. Max hoped that the fire would destroy any evidence of his involvement.

A small figure stood in front of the burned-out house and looked long and hard at it. A deep heat burned within his breast.

Granny Haswell was there tearing at her hair and clothes and crying aloud. Lester put his hand on her shoulder, and she turned sharply at the sudden, cold pressure. Vaguely aware that he was there she whispered, "That you Lester?"

He nodded and realised that she couldn't see him but had sensed his presence.

Granny had been credited with having powers that no one could explain. She was consulted on a variety of things from finding lost items to talking to the departed.

Wilbur Deeds, Sheriff of Calico county pulled up at the burned shell in Canyon Road and saw Fire Chief Dawson looking very closely at the floor.

"Sheriff!" He said tipping his hat.

"Looks like deliberate arson. Marks of an accelerant are there and there." He pointed to the areas in question.

"I think you should take a look at these too!"

In the burnt-out living room were two bodies, both under a tarpaulin. He lifted a corner and almost lost his lunch. Both boys were hardly recognisable as children. Black, soot encrusted corpses the skin around the mouth pulled back in a deathly grimace. But one thing that drew his attention was the gash in the younger boy's neck. The heat had pulled the skin back to reveal a very messy and bloody cut.

Turning his attention to the older boy his shirt was cut and there was a gash in his neck, but his right hand had the fingers hanging by some skin. The Sheriff walked back to his cruiser and took out a small case which contained his camera. He knew enough to take some pictures before the bodies could be removed. He could feel the bile rising into his throat as he snapped the corpses.

Finally, he grunted to the medics who had arrived in response to his radio call to remove the boys to the county morgue for the coroner. Sheriff Deeds found a nearby bush and offloaded his entire stomach contents.

Jessie returned to find her home burned to the ground and Granny Haswell standing on her stoop wringing her hands and weeping.

"Granny? Where are the boys? I can't find them and its past their bedtime!" She looked lost and Granny ran to catch her just as her eyes rolled back into her head and her weight pulled them both down to the ground. Lester watched as it played out in front of him. Sadness came creeping over him including a tinge of regret but most of all there was the rage.

A tall figure in black placed its hand upon his shoulder and a voice echoed in the boy's head.

"I couldn't protect him! Momma trusted me to look after him!" The overwhelming sadness followed by a fierce anger that overtook him again.

"It was the evil within the man that robbed you of your brother! You were a child and will always be so! You are dead Lester but the rage that burns is keeping you here."

"I want to avenge my brother! What can I do if I am dead?" He pleaded.

"You can call upon the power of the rage."

"Look at your hands Lester imagine your nails and your hands have grown stronger and longer!"

Lester looked and thought hard. At first it was a struggle but gradually the anger took over and first one then more fingers started to grow, and the nails curled into claws. He held his hand up and examined the results and felt an obscene pleasure at what he saw.

"Now, think of who did this to your brother?"

Lester tried to remember but the face was vague, blurred, but he felt that being dead was harder than he ever imagined.

An image of a large man with a blonde crewcut started to push through and further images of a skinny, smelly drug addict with a poor choice in clothes running upstairs to look for anything to steal. He also thought of the baby-faced boy that he recognised as the druggist's son and a very quiet girl not much older than himself the look of shock at his brother's demise. Suddenly the image of Frankie pushed right into the forefront of his thoughts.

He was running and about to get on a bus. Lester, thought hard about him and in a heartbeat he appeared beside him.

Frankie felt a cold wet feeling coming over him. He fished into his pocket and withdrew a hand rolled cigarette and lit it the air filled with a pungent aroma.

"Put that out!" Shouted the driver and Frankie took one last pull from it before putting it out. He held the smoke in his mouth for a time and released it into his lungs. He turned to look out of the windows and came face to face with Lester.

His eyes were rolled back showing the whites and the gash in his neck bled profusely. Frankie let out a scream as Lester brought his claw hand up to pass through his clothes and take hold of Frankie's beating heart and gradually squeezed it until it stopped.

Everyone heard the scream and turned as one in their seats and saw Frankie slide down in an empty seat. The driver stopped the bus and went back to check on him. He placed two fingers on his neck – no pulse! Totally dead!

Sheriff Deeds was called to the death on the coach.

Granny Haswell sat watching Jessie's breathing as she laid on Granny's couch.

Lester returned to his old home and felt a pull toward Granny's house. He somehow knew that his mother was there, and he let it pull him through Granny's door. His mother was lying fast asleep and in a dream state he found himself inside her head he saw her crying and holding her arms out to him.

He walked toward her showing her a perfect vision of himself. He let her hold him in the dream state for a time and she realised he was gone. Leaving behind him a loving feeling she woke to find herself in Granny's.

"He was here chile!" Granny told her. "Ah felt him in here around us!" She continued.

"Granny, he was in my dream, I held him for the last time. I got to say goodbye to my babies. But Charlie wasn't there! Why wasn't he there Granny?" Jessie sobbed.

"Well! It looks like Charlie went over easier but Lester, well Lester don't want to go just yet. Got somethin to do first?"

"How do you know? "

"Well, he talk to me he pull my skirt or put his hand on my shoulder, and he whisper in my ear!"

"He said one done three more to go?"

"What is that supposed to mean? "Jessie looked puzzled.

Wilbur sat back in his chair with his feet up on his desk. Deputy Will Collins came in with a file and put it on his desk.

"Will, I was getting comfortable there got my tilt angle jest right an now I have to pick up that file son!"

"Want me to hand it to yu Sheriff? It's the coroner's report on those poor kids at Canyon Road!"

Wilbur straightened himself up, the joking stopped the smile wiped off as he picked up the report. "Seems like it was murder, jest like I figured, and a fire set to destroy evidence! Some defensive wounds on the older boy's hands and the gashes and stab wounds all point to a hunter's blade twelve inches long serrated one side and smooth on the other. But one thing missing from this report – motive! Why would anyone kill kids?"

"I know it's not the coroner's job to provide a motive, but t darn it, what have we to go on here?" Will stroked his chin for a moment and was about to offer a theory but paused.

"Spit it out son! You wanna say something?"

"Well, it would be hard to tell if it was robbery! House being caved in an all. But in my mind you don't have to kill anyone lessen they could identify ya, so he/they were wearing masks Sheriff?"

"Dammit son that's good reasoning."

"But have we any suspects at this point – no!"

"No but what we do have is boot prints leaving the house and a dark patch in the dust that has proved to be paraffin oil that was tracked out?" Will pointed out, "I took a plaster cast of one of the bootprints and it was a size ten and it had a worn heel on the outside edge with a crack in it. I also reckon that this was a big guy from the stride distance Sheriff."

Will continued, "there were about four people there and one was a woman. Those prints were a bit broken up, but I think I could find more"

"Ok Will see what you can find a bit further out from the house."

The coroner had a body on his slab that had seen better days. "He was 6ft 3. Fingernails were fairly clean, clothes that hung in rags in places on him. A belt cinched tightly around his waist taking up the slack in his large sized pants. His boots were in reasonable shape – size ten, worn down at the outside edge of the heel and about to split through with a crack."

Dr. Willerson County Coroner was making his initial first impressions known to his assistant Ben Tillman who was transcribing onto a lined notepad. "Right Ben, making my 'Y' incision now! Pulling rib cage apart to take a look at his heart – holy shit! Would ya look at this?"

As Ben looked in he could see that the heart had been shredded.

"In all my years as both Dr and Coroner I aint never seen something like this! How the hell can you shred a heart without marking the damn outside. If I didn't know any better I would say it had been mauled by a lion or a damn bear!"

The paperwork landed on Wilbur's desk. As he read the report he called Will on the radio.
"Will, have you managed to get anymore bootprints yet?"
"Yeah I shure did, much clearer further out in fact right on the edge of Canyon Road a group of people stood in a ring an I got casts of everyone."
"Well hightail it back here son – I think we caught a break in this case!"
Wilbur read though the Coroner's report on the drug addict and through his fingerprints identified as one Frankie Duchesne. Frankie was in the system for dealing drugs, using and for carrying a concealed weapon, namely one crowbar.
Will compared his boots with the casts taken from the scene. The cracked boot clinched it. He had been there but they both knew that without proper evidence it could be purely coincidental.

Lester, working his power rage, found Max Quigley.
Quigley was sitting in Dixie's bar on main street in his usual place with a bottle of bourbon in front of him. He had heard of Frankie Duchesne's sudden

demise. Max had decided to drown his sorrows and he tossed glass after glass down his throat.

After his fifth glass he was shocked to see Lester sitting across from him.

"Aw fuck man you seeing things now!" He said to himself.

"You recognise me now Quigley?" Lester whispered in his ear and opened up the tear in his neck and blood squirted profusely over Quigley's jacket. He tried vainly to brush it off with a napkin but the more he tried blood just flowed more.
Several people in the bar watched in fascination as he furiously scrubbed at nothing on his coat.

Lester lifted up the claws that were his hands and reaching out scooped out Max Quigley's eyes. The patrons were shocked to see the eyes pop out seemingly by themselves and gouge lines appearing on his face.

Finally, a claw struck him just under his chin ripping out his windpipe and splitting his jugular to send his life force across the wet table.

As one, the patrons made a dash for the door. Ladies tripped and fell, others in panic fell over them crushing the people who were unlucky enough to lose their footing.

The energy of Lester's rage started to abate, and he was pulled back to his home. As new energy flowed back to replenish him, he saw Granny sitting in her rocker. He glided up the stairs and whispered two done, two more to go.

"Lester! What are you doing boy?" She said to the cold air around her.

"Revenge! Granny – revenge! They killed Charlie and me, now I have killed two of them! I want to make Momma proud?"
Granny was about to answer him, but he winked out of the conversation.

Opie was next on his list and Lester knew just where he would find him! At home with his
Dad. Opie was scared stiff as he sat hunched up and tense in the armchair.

"Darn it Opie what's gotten into you?" Said Bill Cleveland.

"Dad! I gotta level with ya. Those two kids that were killed, it was Max Quigley. He cut them and killed them I was with them, but I never done nothing just watched is all!" He stammered.

Bill Cleveland jumped out of his chair and slapped Opie so hard the noise was like a thunderclap, and he toppled sideways from the chair.

"You twisted little shit! Haven't I given you a good home and everything you ever wanted since your Ma passed on? Well? Haven't I?" He paused, "Yes Pa!" He whispered looking down at his feet.

Bill moved to the side table and picked up the phone he dialled and waited.

"Sheriff's office Gina speaking?"

"Gina! Tell Wilbur I need to see him as soon as he can at my house!"

"Can you tell me what it is about?"

"No best for his ears only!" Bill hung up.

Gina went to the shortwave radio that was on the desk near her. It crackled into life as she relayed Bill's message. Wilbur acknowledged the message and put the microphone back on its hook.

He wondered if he should go for a coffee at the local diner first before seeing Bill, but something nagged at the back of his mind. Bill sounded agitated a mite Gina had said and that Wilbur was required as soon as possible.

The sheriff decided to get over to Bill's place now. Bill had the house behind the store and as Wilbur arrived the curtain moved slightly to let a chink of light escape temporarily lighting up the porch. Wilbur hurried up the steps his boots pounding at each one.

The door opened as he raised his hand to knock.

"Come in sheriff been waiting for you!"

He showed him into the parlour where a very nervous Opie sat wringing his hands.

"Ok Bill you have my undivided attention – now what's all the rush?" He removed his hat and took a seat.

"Opie tell the sheriff what you just told me!" He looked at his son.

"Ok but you cannot protect me neither of you! "He sobbed.

"The two kids that were killed sheriff, it was a guy named Max Quigley and his pal Frankie Duchesne, well Frankie was looking for some money or something he could sell for drugs. Max got little Charlie by the neck to force Lester to tell them where it was hid but when he found out there wasn't any he hauled off and hit Charlie with a big ole knife he carried darn near took his head off. Then Lester tried to get the knife from Max and grabbed it, but it was so sharp his fingers were cut through.
Me and Coraline were horrified at what we saw so we legged it outta there – honest we did!"

Wilbur couldn't believe what he was hearing. Opie Cleveland a boy who he watched growing up getting mixed up with Max Quigley and Frankie Duchesne.

"And I am ashamed to say this sheriff, but Opie has been stealing drugs from me – didn't think I knew did you boy? "Opie started to cry and pleaded with Bill and the sheriff not to send him to jail.

"Out of my hands now boy gonna let the sheriff deal with you now!" Bill looked cold and hard at Opie. "Your Ma would be ashamed of you for doing this evil thing!"

The door swung open by itself, and footsteps echoed as they entered the room. Wilbur drew his gun but could not see anything or anyone to shoot. Lester stood directly in front of Opie and looked into his frightened eyes.

Lacerations appeared from groin to chest opening him up like a letter. His entrails spilled out onto the floor in a bloody steaming pile.

Opie looked down as his intestine fell and then he too followed the bloody mess to the ground his screams made all of the neighbours looking out of their windows nervously from behind twitching curtains. Then the door slammed closed, the invisible footsteps receded down the hall and into the night.

Bill looked down at the deflated corpse of his son and wept. He knew in his heart that his boy was just misguided but didn't need to have this done to him. He was prepared to send him to jail to get straightened out but this, this was something else. Wilbur hurried to his cruiser and retrieved his camera and took pictures for evidence.

Only thing he thought was – "How the fuck can I put this down in my report? Who would believe that an invisible assailant tore young Opie apart, while me his Pa were right there in the god damn room and did fuck all to stop it – well how could we deal with something supernatural?"

Wilbur paused in his thought and decided he needed to consult someone who was more favourable to working in the realms of the supernatural – Granny Haswell.

Sheriff pulled up outside Granny's house and walked up the wooden steps and knocked on her door. His knock echoed within the building. At first he was about to turn round and go home but the door opened slowly a crack until the one surveying eye flung open the door wide.

"Why Sheriff Deeds have you come a courting ole Granny?" She cackled and laughed at her little joke until it made her cough again.

"Darn cough spoils my fun!"

"What can I do fer ya Sheriff? "

"Call me Wilbur Granny, I need your advice on the er um the other worldly realms so to speak!" He held his hat in front of him.

"Come in an set awhile Wilbur. I take it you met with somethin beyond your reckoning?" She leaned forward and stared at the Sheriff.

"Yep Granny, we sure did. While I was talking to Opie Cleveland he just split right up from belly to neck you might say. Oh an before that a door opened by itself and sounds of footsteps walked right up to him. Now you realise that you cannot discuss this with anyone else outside of here right?"

Granny nodded.

"Well, I have a notion it was young Lester doing it Sheriff!" Granny said matter of factly.

"But Lester is dead!"

"Yep, but that boy has a rage, an unholy anger and a lust for revenge! He told me so earlier that he done two an two more to go?"

"Are you sure this is right? I mean how can a 'spirit/ghost or whatever kill someone from beyond the grave?" Wilbur was having a hard time trying to get his head round this information.

"Well, my Mammy an her Mammy before that were sensitive shall we say to the spirit world. We could talk to them and get them through their passing which can be hard if they meet a bad end. Just like Lester. But young Charlie now he was different he wuz an innocent chile that just went over quickly. Lester, now he was given a chore to do, he promised to protect an look after Charlie but before he could Charlie wuz killed and Lester well he feels a powerful guilt that needs to punish those who took his little brother.

His last words to me were he was gonna make his Momma proud!" Granny watched Wilbur assimilate this information.

"I have to admit Granny it makes a lot of sense to me now. The other members of the gang involved have been taken out, Frankie Duchesne, Max Quigley, Opie Cleveland. But one thing bothers me – there was a young woman name of Coraline Rivers. We haven't been able to find her yet but given Lester's power, she is gonna be next? When and where and can we stop Lester killing her?"

Granny paused removed her glasses and rubbed the bridge of her nose, "I seem to remember the feel of his presence and his voice dropped to a whisper after he had taken one. I am betting that he has to return to his ole house to recharge, he gets his power from the rage in the house where it happened!"

"Then we have a couple of hours to search for Coraline Rivers and do we need silver bullets or a cross to stop him Granny?" Wilbur asked. Granny laughed "Boy not a werewolf so no bullets of silver and he is a ghost not a vampire either, so a cross won't do a thing to him. Maybe a good talking to by yours truly and his Momma might turn him back to righteousness.

As Lester, wandered around the burned-out house he was finding it harder to rage against the killing of his brother. Was there a satisfaction in having removed the killers but at the back of his 'mind' there was a little doubt regarding the last one, Opie.

Lester pictured the scene of the killing, seeing it all playing as if he was in the movie theatre. How Opie had looked shocked when he had opened the door and saw Lester trying to fight off Max. He hadn't tried to stop Max from taking his life no matter how shocked so therefore he was guilty by association Lester reasoned that was how the law worked. He felt a bit better at this thought.

The rage flamed again. This time he knew that the girl was also guilty by association.

As such she was now sentenced to die at his 'hands.'

Coraline, read in the papers of the strange deaths of two people. As soon as she read their names she knew she was free at last. Free from the abuse that Max had heaped upon her day after day. Trouble was going to find her, and she knew it. When or where she didn't know but it was coming.

Perhaps she should give herself up to the law and maybe get a shorter sentence. She hadn't stabbed or murdered those kids. She was forced to go along and witness the whole horrific thing. She had nightmares ever since.

"Yes that's what I'll do I shall give myself up and fall upon the mercy of the court!" Coraline walked fast toward the Sheriff's office and walked through the double glass doors. There was a hum in the background like she was in a hive with worker bees. All buzzing around and moving from one place to another.

She approached a young woman in a silk blouse and thought what a pretty shade of pink. The young lady looked up. "Can I help you Ma'am?" she trilled.

"I want to have a word with the Sheriff please!"

"Ok who shall I say wants him? Miss er?"

"Coraline Rivers, I think he might wish to speak to me quite urgently?" She paused.

"I shall wait here, shall I?" Coraline sat next to the water cooler. Stood up, took a paper cup and put water in an gulped it down her throat. She had all of a sudden become very parched.

Lester, sat in the seat next to her. He debated whether or not to strike her down in the Sheriff's office. Something was messing with his power it was wavering from strong too weak to strong again.

A powerful wave of energy drew him to the double doors and there on the threshold was his Momma and old Granny Haswell.

"Lester, son I know you are here, Granny told me. We want to talk to you! Come to Granny with me!" The power that came from Granny was irresistible and he found he was alongside her now.

"Lester, your Momma knows you made a promise, but you got the killers, and she is mighty proud of you boy. The young lady made out a statement that she was outside the house she never saw what you did for Charlie only the bodies that Max tried to burn.

"Revenge is a powerful rage son, but forgiveness is also powerful. You can go on to the light if you can forgive her?"

The energy was pulling him apart and the rage was weakening. What would he do when the rage had gone? What had Granny said?, forgiveness was a power too and he could go on.
At that moment Granny heard him say I forgive her; she also heard him say goodbye Momma gonna go find Charlie.

Lester, the ghost boy disappeared.
Granny and Jessie explained what had happened to Lester and that he was finally purged.

Coraline, related how Max had abused her and that she had been so afraid of him that she felt trapped by him. The jury found her guilty by association but recommended clemency for mitigation purposes. She served one year of a two-year sentence.

Received parole and lived out her days in Calico County.

The Whistling Slasher

Annie Wilson gazed into her fire; the warm glow highlighted her care-worn face. Her only companions were two mongrels, since her children had grown up and left home.

The only sounds she heard were the steady tick of her old clock on the mantelpiece and the "snick-snick" of the dogs' claws upon the linoleum, as they went to their water bowls.

Annie had lived most of her life in a little cottage, which nestled on the outskirts of Ainthorpe village. A village that her children had later found boring and lifeless.

She turned on the radio, her nightly ritual before bed. The newscaster interrupted her programme with a special bulletin.

"Early this morning, a dangerous criminal - John Oaks, escaped from Parklands Sanatorium for the criminally insane - do not approach this man! Oaks - is also known as the 'Whistling Slasher' bolt all doors and windows, now back to the programme."

Annie shivered at the thought of this man roaming the countryside, and that Parklands was a mere eight miles away.

"Too far away from here to worry over," she chided herself, "probably long gone by now!"

However, she still tentatively went to check the security of her doors and windows. As she reached her back door, the darkness was dispelled bright flash of lightning, followed by a deep, booming thunderclap. She jumped at the unexpected sound. Rain fell in sheets, drumming on the roof of her primitive dwelling.

"I should have had electricity put in years ago," She said. Her dogs cowered in the dark as the storm broke overhead.

"Some protection you are!" She laughed, "imagine being afraid of a storm."

All she got in reply were whimpers. She lit her oil lamp, ready for retiring, and then took it to light her way to bed. She dragged her frail body up the gruelling flight of stairs that led to her tiny bedroom at the front of the house.

Having set the lamp on her nightstand, she prepared herself for bed. She listened to the storm raging and to the susurrus of the trees amid the constant drumming of the rain on the roof. Annie drifted off to the sound of the rain. She woke with a start, in the early hours. Sweat droplets formed on her top lip. She wiped them off with her sleeve - she lay back, and then instinctively dropped her hand out of the bed. Annie sought the reassurance of her dogs, which were inclined to take up residence under the bed, and to lick her hand when it came near.

She hadn't the heart to send them downstairs and so had allowed them to sleep in her room overnight. She felt the comforting response of a wet tongue on her hand and promptly went back to sleep. When she awoke, she could hear drops of liquid falling.

"Must be stopping now," she thought, "all that rain will have ruined my flowers."

Annie made her way to the bathroom for a shower – there - hung up - were the two dogs, their throats had been cut and the blood dripped into the bath.

On the bathroom mirror, written in their blood was the message...

Not only dogs can lick hands!

Her hands flew to her face in horror, as she read it.

The last thing that Annie heard was a tuneless whistle as the razor entered her old, white neck, stifling her wordless scream.

About the Author

Born in 1948 and residing in Middlesbrough, UK, Paul had an ambition to see his name in print but left it until now to actually do it. So having it as an item on a bucket list was the next best thing. His past influences have been Stephen King, Dean Koontz and Richard Laymon and his present influences Kelvin VA Allison, Mark Green and Lee Richmond. Paul has also been known to dabble in pen-making, leatherworking and photography.

Printed in Great Britain
by Amazon

45508652R00101